BIRD·BOY

Volume II: The Liminal Wood

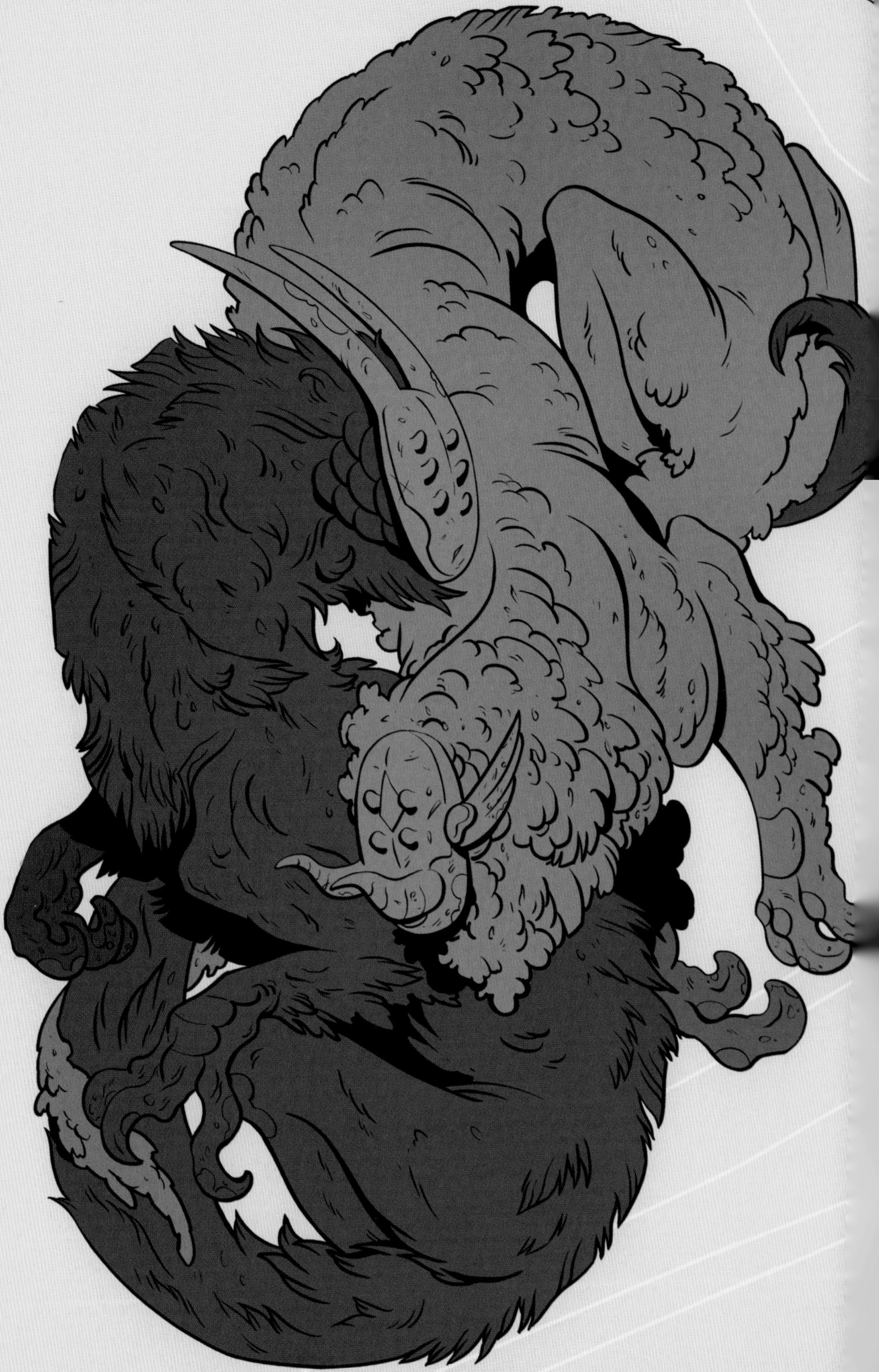

BIRD·BOY ™

VOLUME II: THE LIMINAL WOOD

DARK HORSE BOOKS

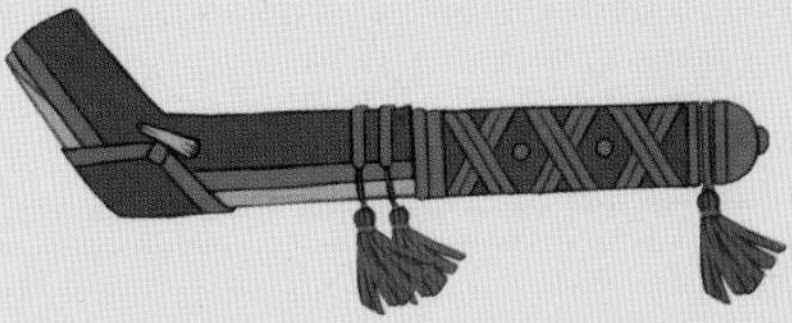

President and Publisher
Mike Richardson

Editor
Scott Allie

Associate Editor
Shantel LaRocque

Assistant Editor
Katii O'Brien

Collection Designer
Sandy Tanaka

Digital Art Technician
Christianne Goudreau

Neil Hankerson Executive Vice President • **Tom Weddle** Chief Financial Officer • **Randy Stradley** Vice President of Publishing • **Michael Martens** Vice President of Book Trade Sales • **Matt Parkinson** Vice President of Marketing • **David Scroggy** Vice President of Product Development • **Dale LaFountain** Vice President of Information Technology • **Cara Niece** Vice President of Production and Scheduling • **Nick McWhorter** Vice President of Media Licensing • **Ken Lizzi** General Counsel • **Dave Marshall** Editor in Chief • **Davey Estrada** Editorial Director • **Scott Allie** Executive Senior Editor • **Chris Warner** Senior Books Editor • **Cary Grazzini** Director of Print and Development • **Lia Ribacchi** Art Director • **Mark Bernardi** Director of Digital Publishing • **Michael Gombos** Director of International Publishing and Licensing

Published by Dark Horse Books
A division of Dark Horse Comics, Inc.
10956 SE Main Street
Milwaukie, OR 97222

First edition: August 2016
ISBN 978-1-61655-968-7

1 3 5 7 9 10 8 6 4 2
Printed in China

Bird-Boy.com

International Licensing: (503) 905-2377 Comic Shop Locator Service: (888) 266-4226

Bird Boy Volume 2: The Liminal Wood

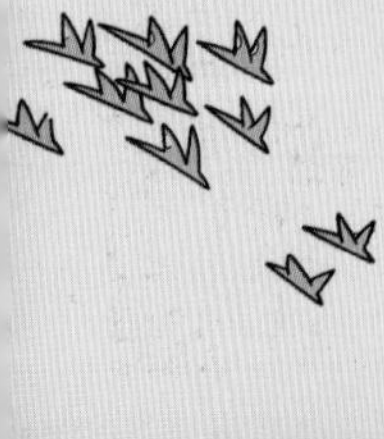

Library of Congress Cataloging-in-Publication data is available

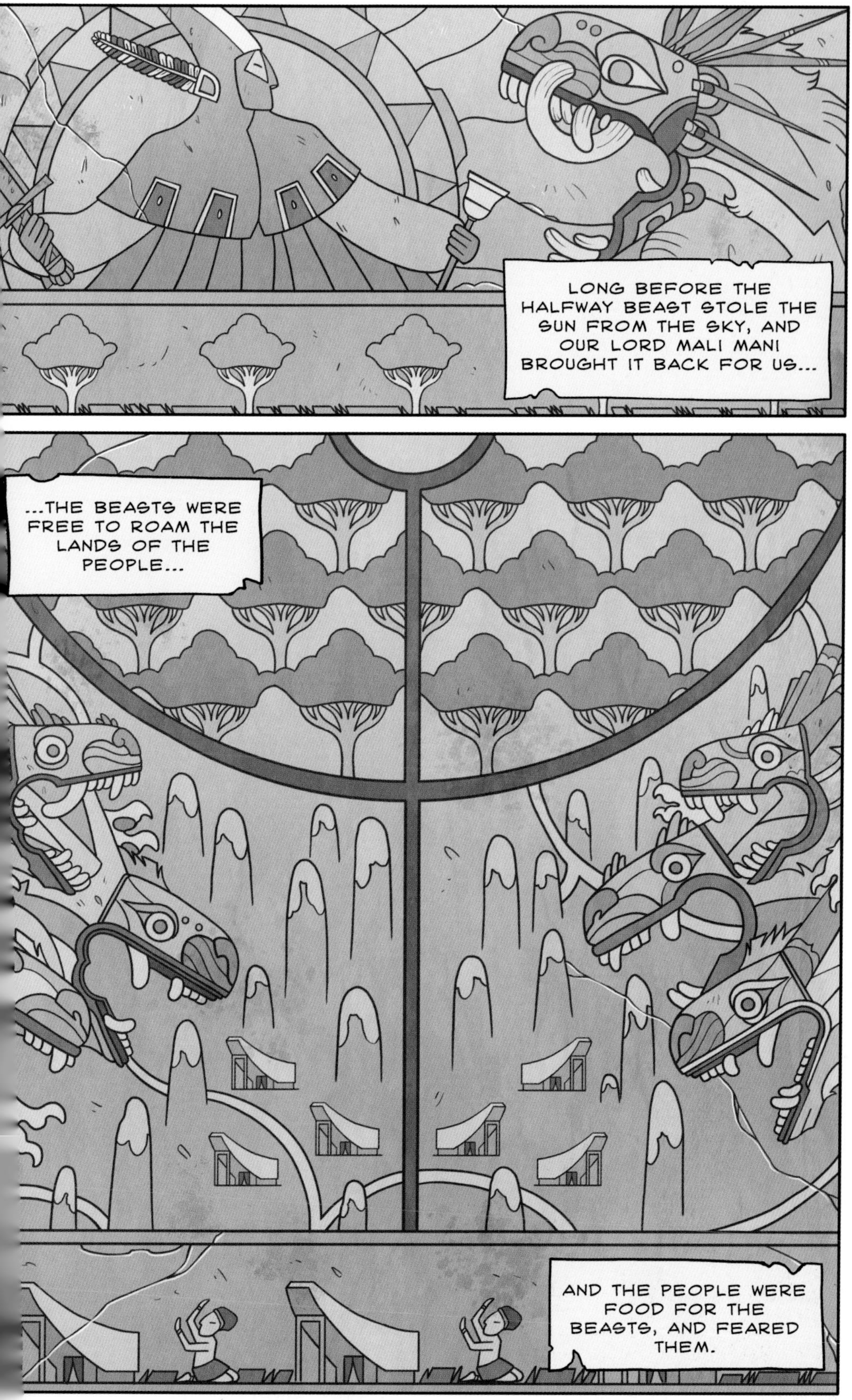
LONG BEFORE THE HALFWAY BEAST STOLE THE SUN FROM THE SKY, AND OUR LORD MALI MANI BROUGHT IT BACK FOR US...
...THE BEASTS WERE FREE TO ROAM THE LANDS OF THE PEOPLE...
AND THE PEOPLE WERE FOOD FOR THE BEASTS, AND FEARED THEM.

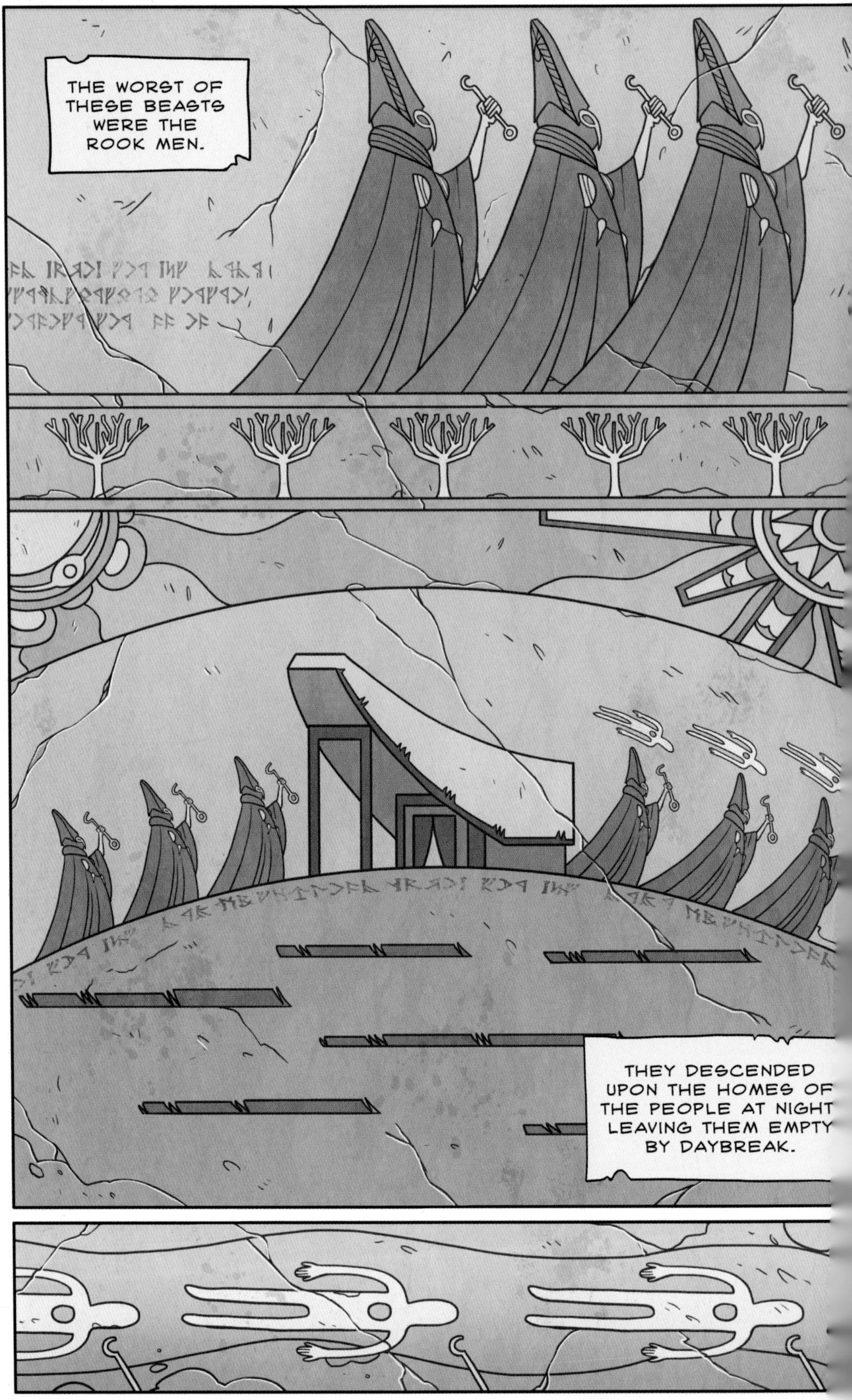
THE WORST OF THESE BEASTS WERE THE ROOK MEN.
THEY DESCENDED UPON THE HOMES OF THE PEOPLE AT NIGHT LEAVING THEM EMPTY BY DAYBREAK.

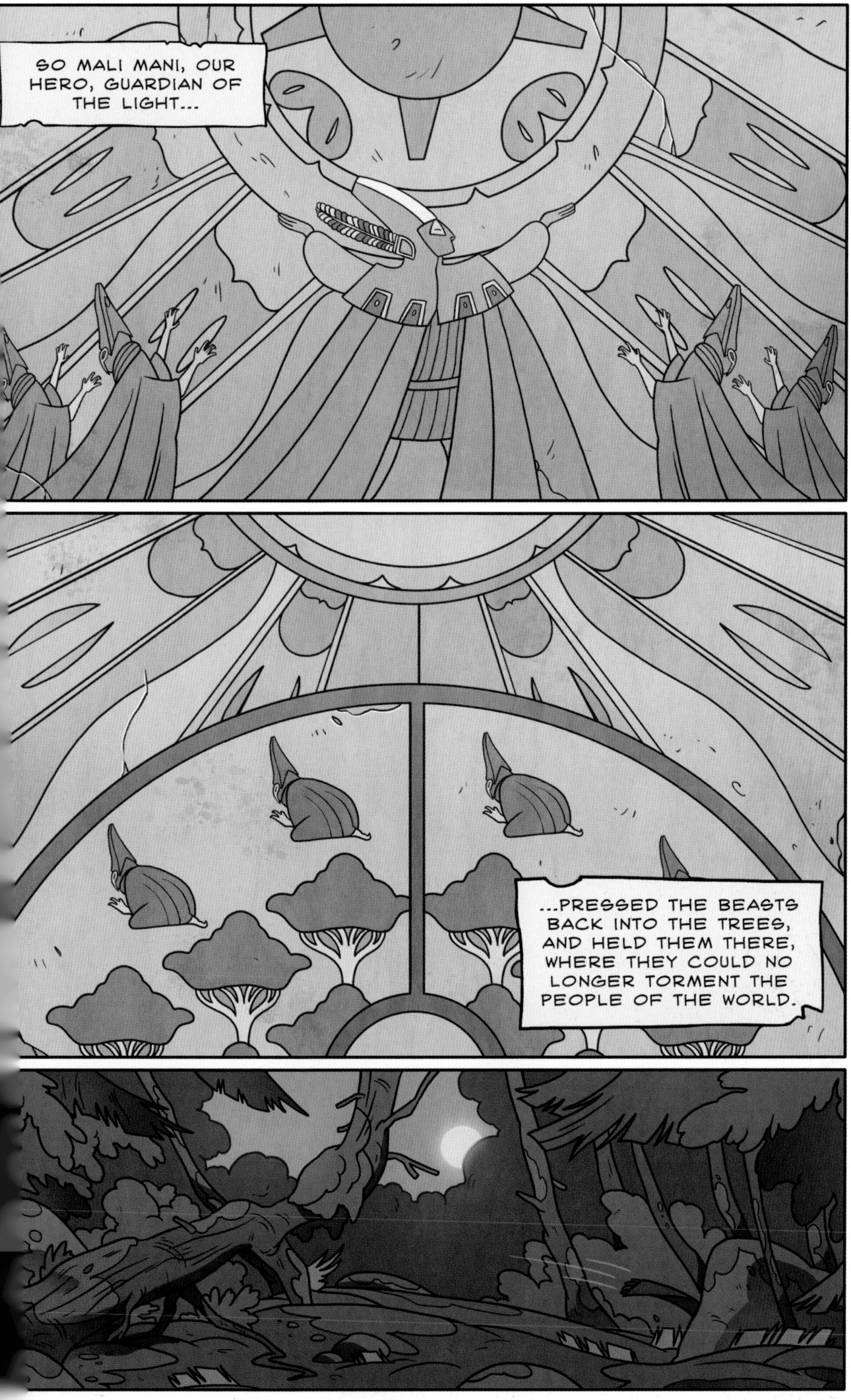
SO MALI MANI, OUR HERO, GUARDIAN OF THE LIGHT...
...PRESSED THE BEASTS BACK INTO THE TREES, AND HELD THEM THERE, WHERE THEY COULD NO LONGER TORMENT THE PEOPLE OF THE WORLD.

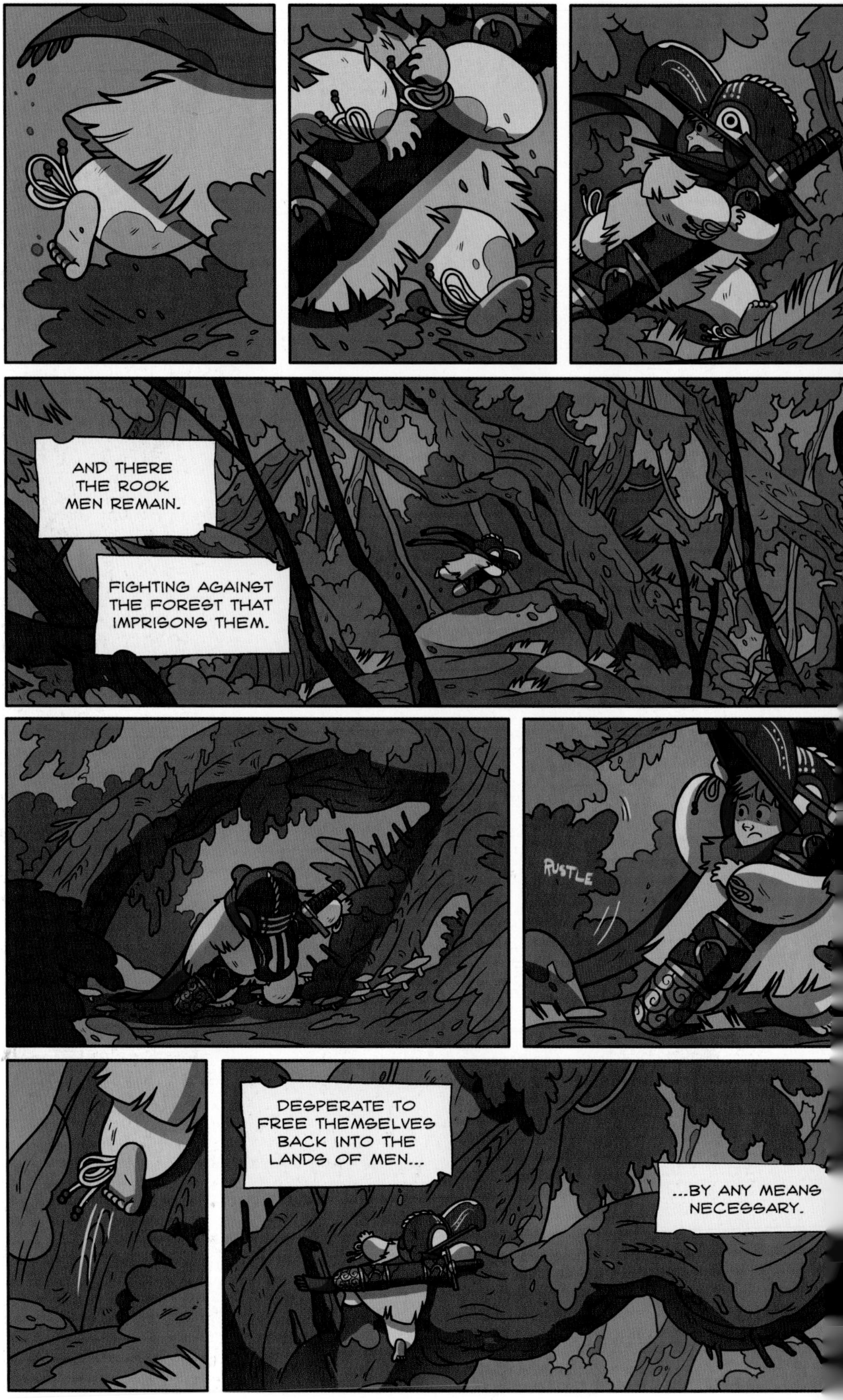
AND THERE THE ROOK MEN REMAIN.
FIGHTING AGAINST THE FOREST THAT IMPRISONS THEM.
RUSTLE
DESPERATE TO FREE THEMSELVES BACK INTO THE LANDS OF MEN...
...BY ANY MEANS NECESSARY.

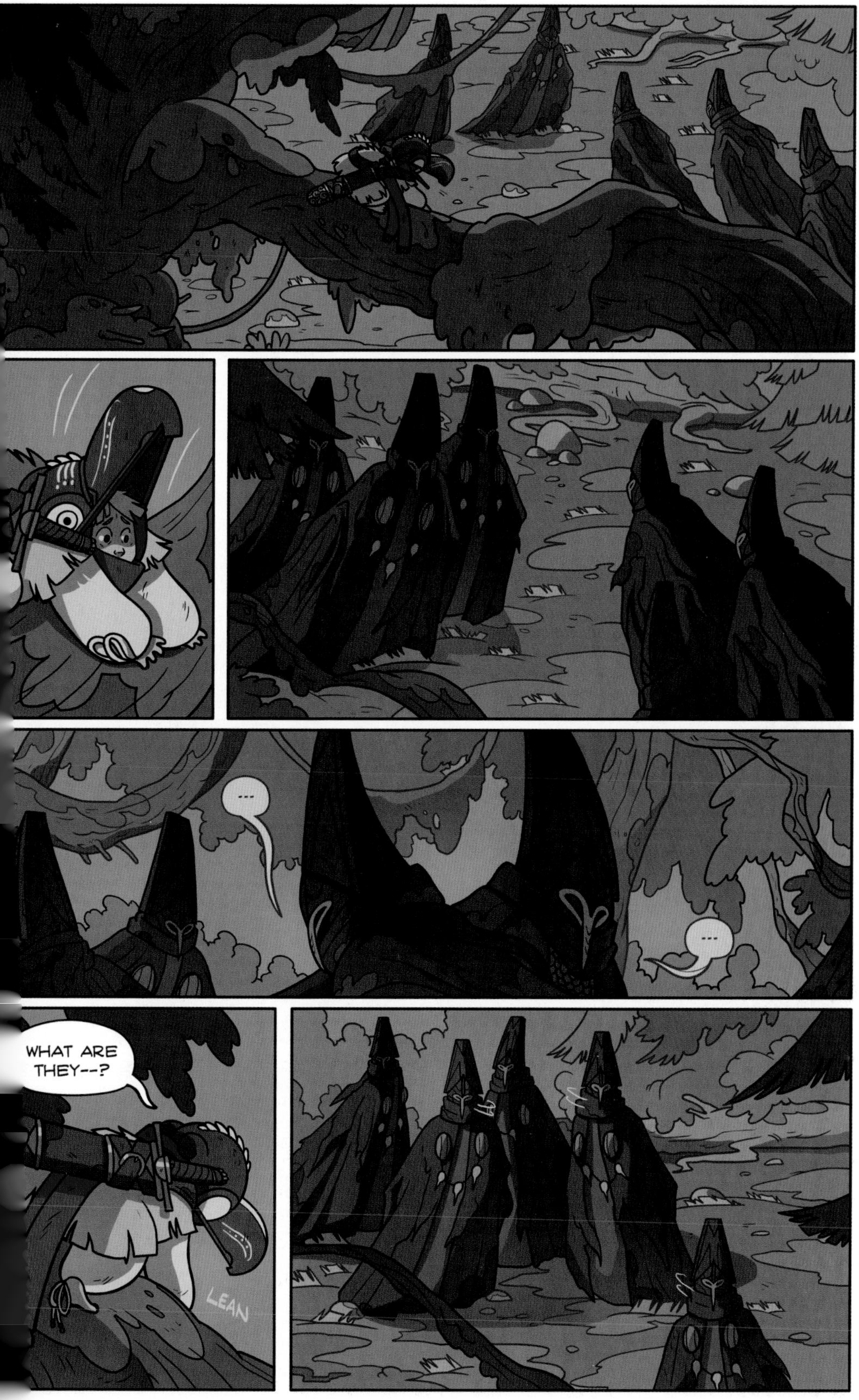
...
...
WHAT ARE THEY--?
LEAN

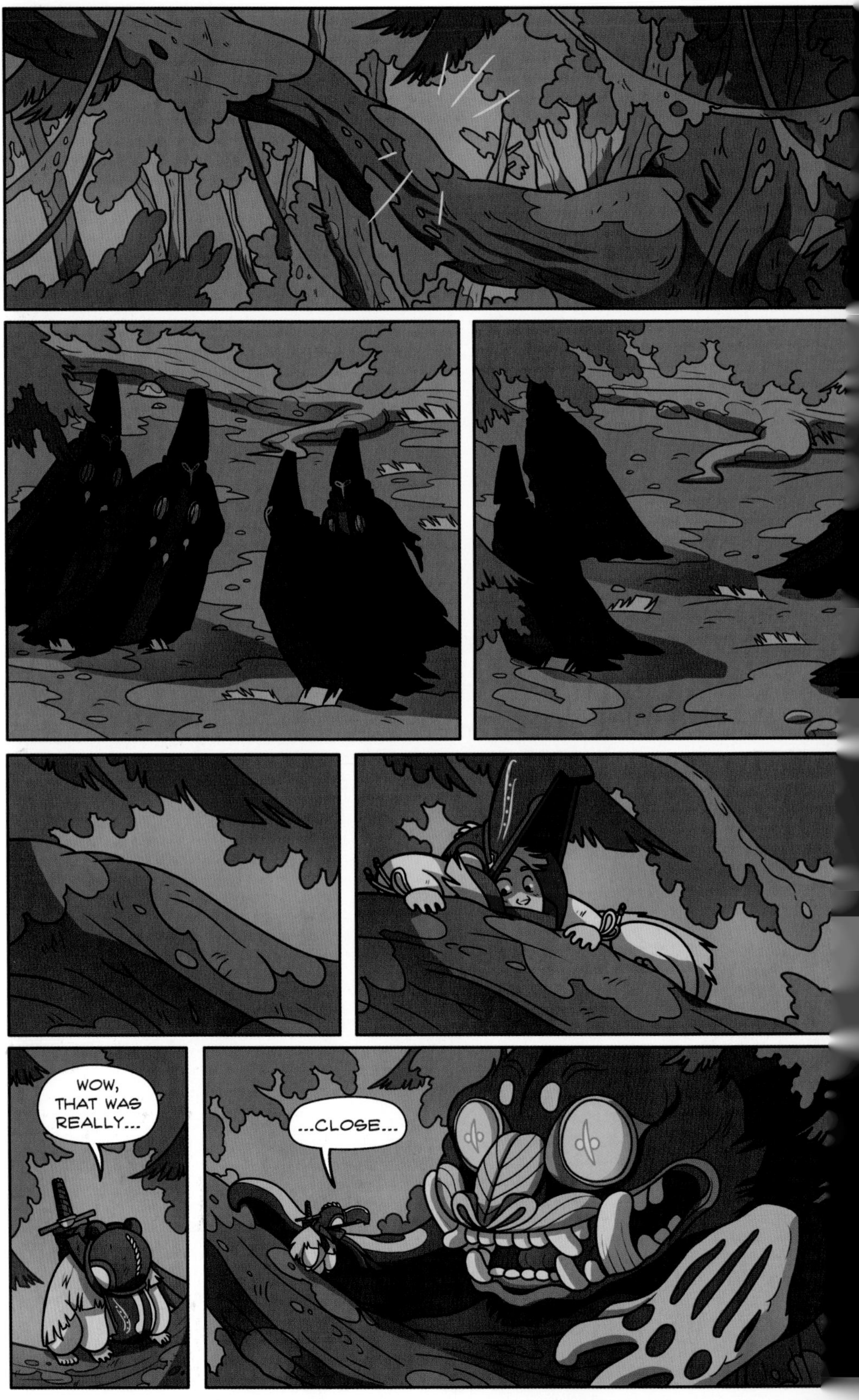
WOW, THAT WAS REALLY...
...CLOSE...

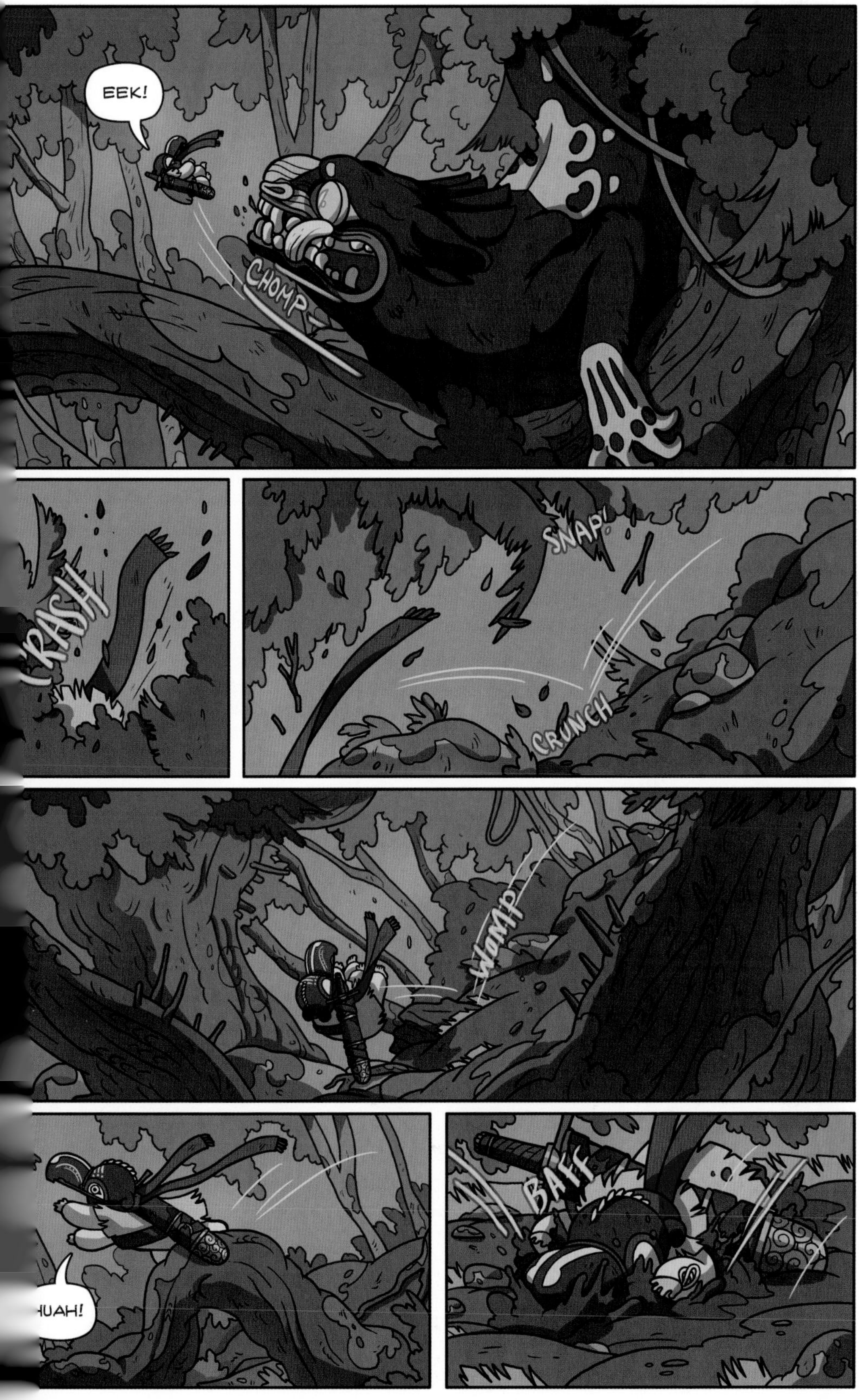
EEK!
CHOMP
CRASH
SNAP!
CRUNCH
WOMP
HUAH!
BAFF

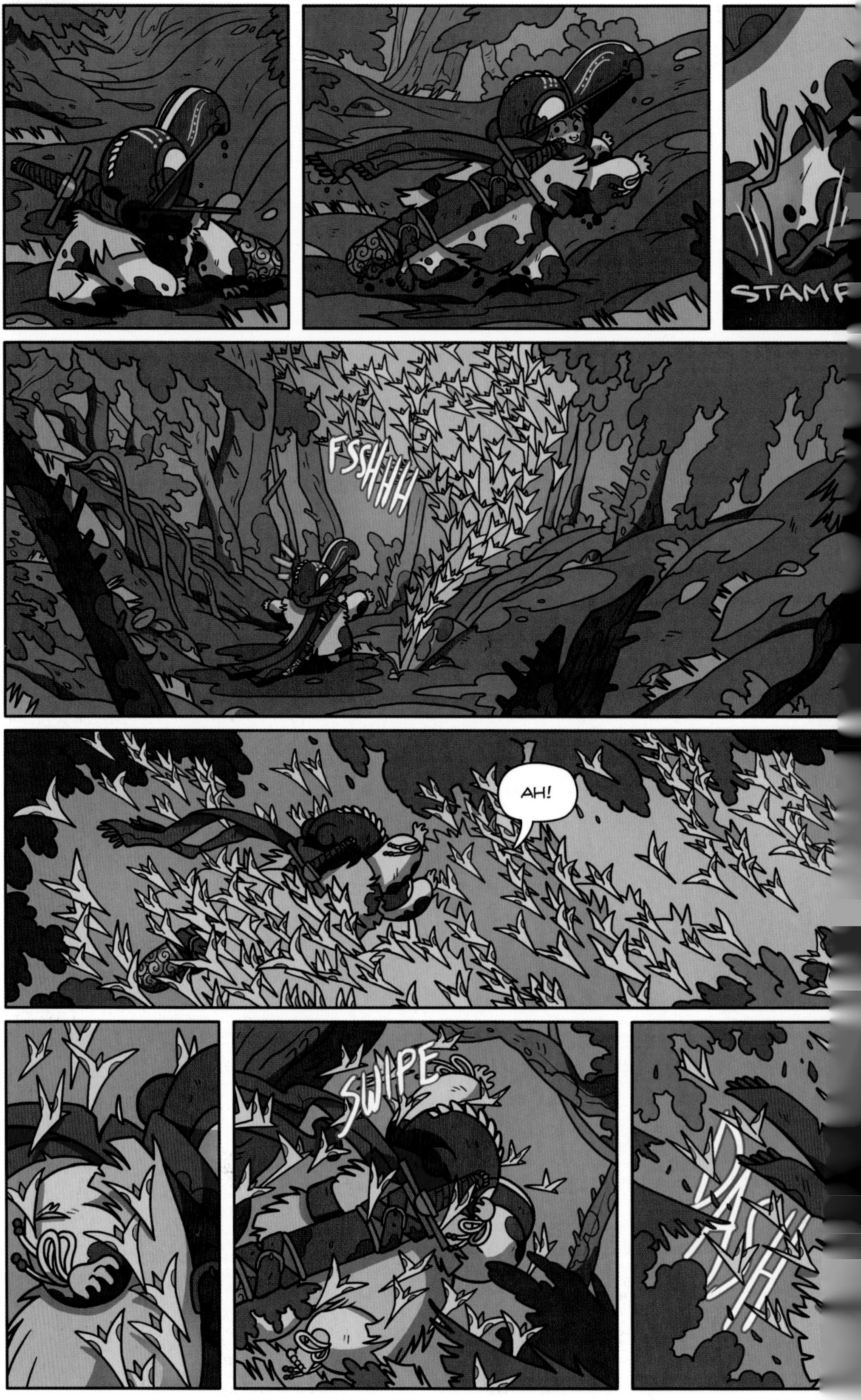
STAMP
FSSHHH
AH!
SWIPE
DASH

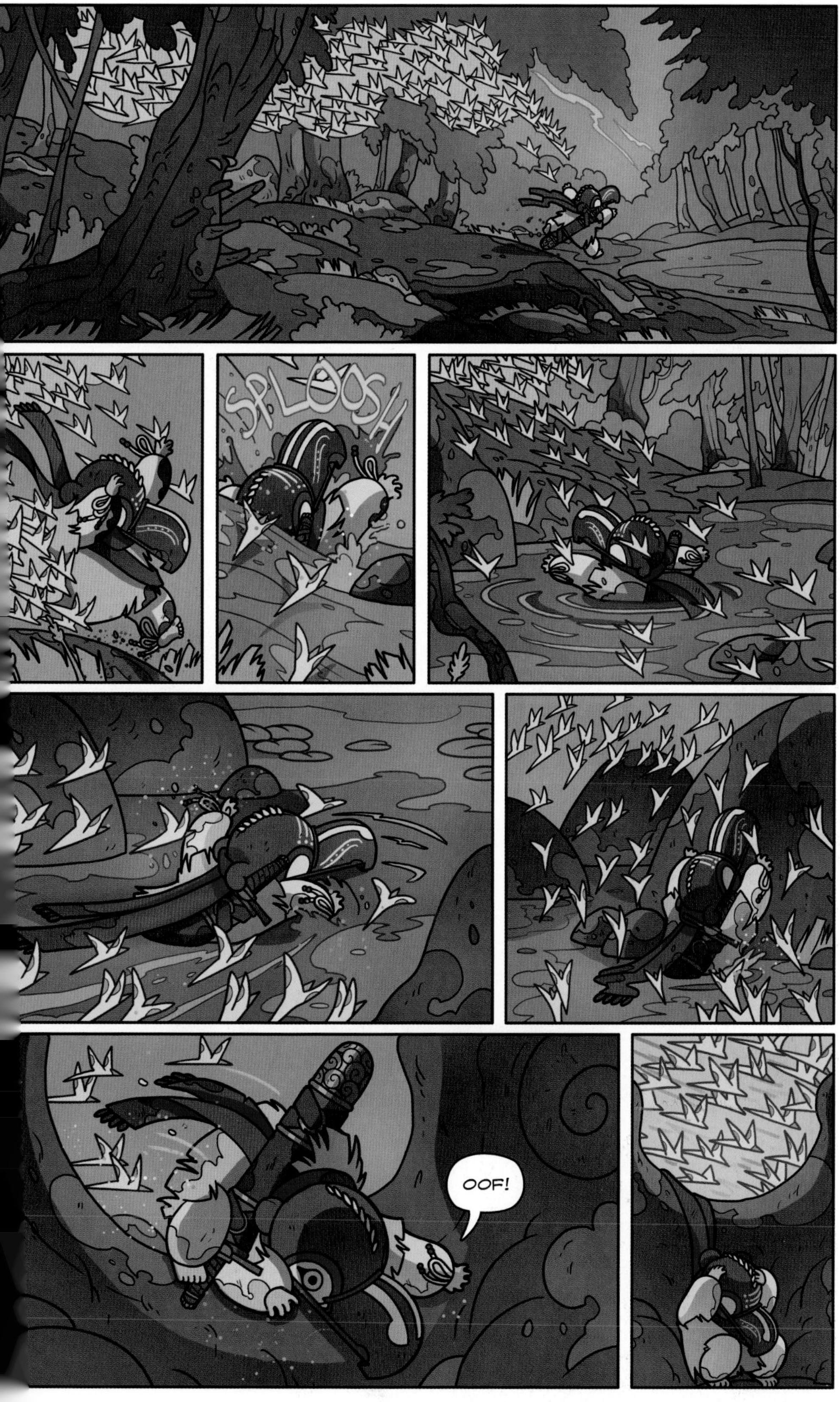
SPLOOSH
OOF!

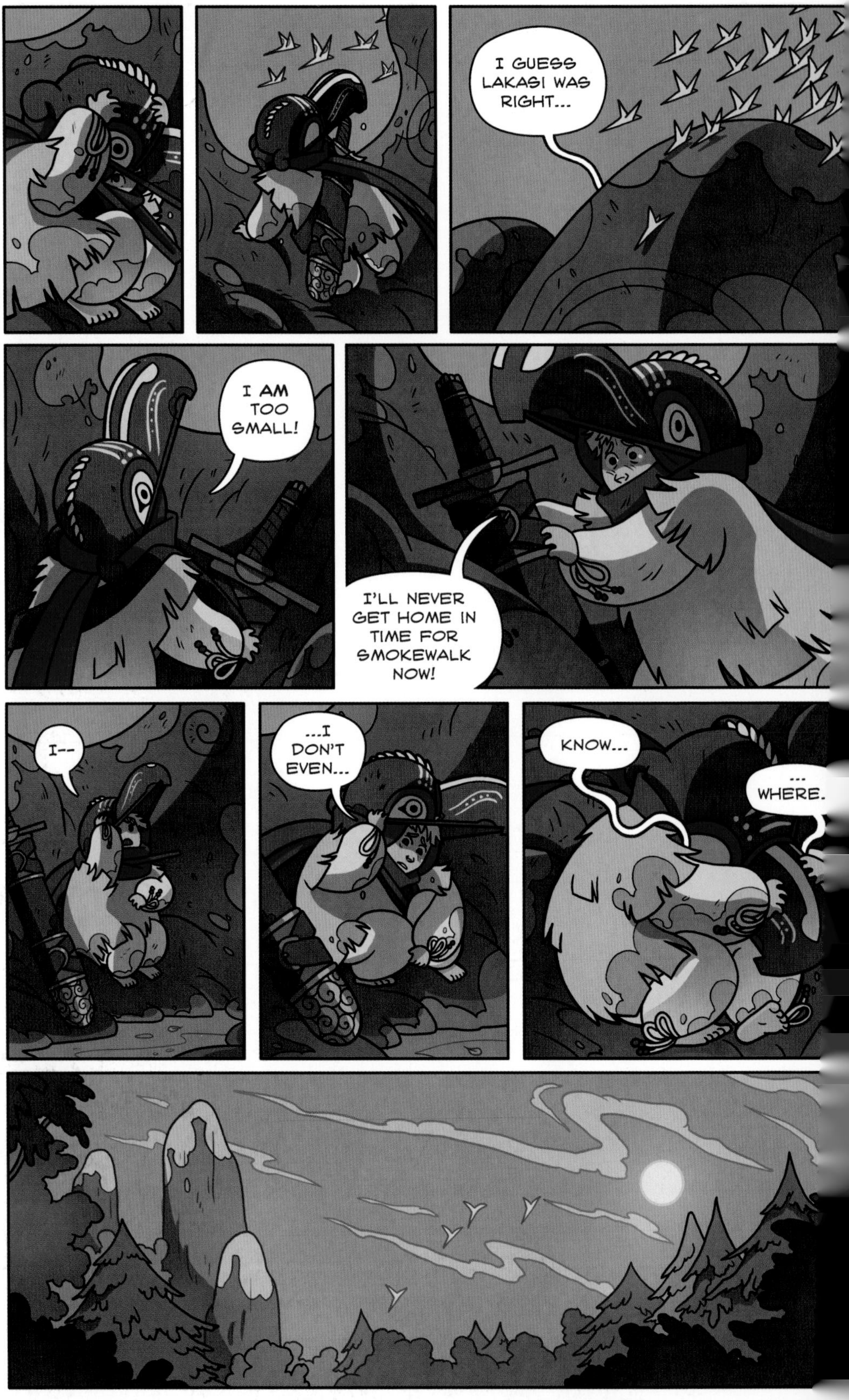
I GUESS LAKASI WAS RIGHT...
I AM TOO SMALL!
I'LL NEVER GET HOME IN TIME FOR SMOKEWALK NOW!
I--
...I DON'T EVEN...
KNOW...
... WHERE.

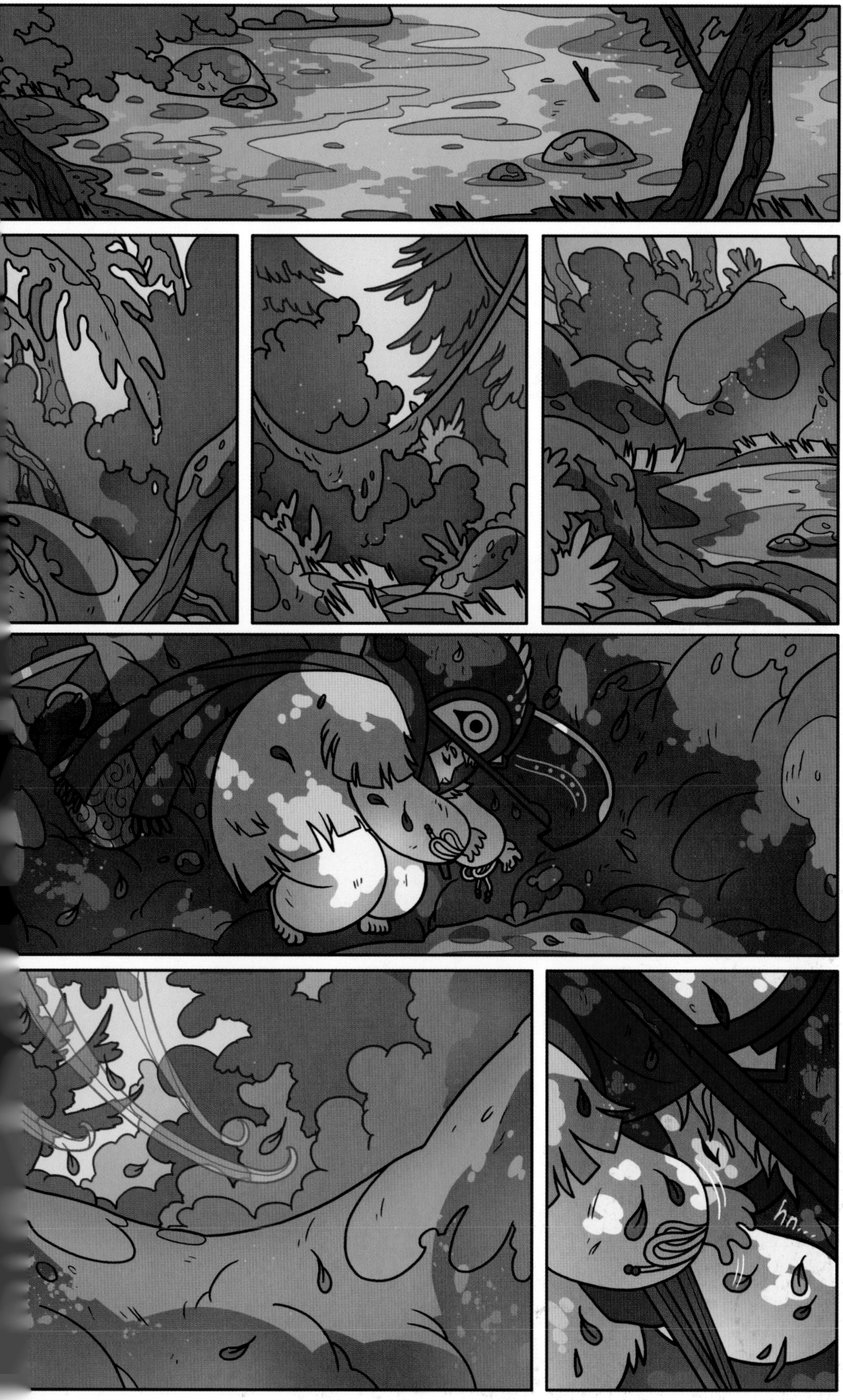
hn...

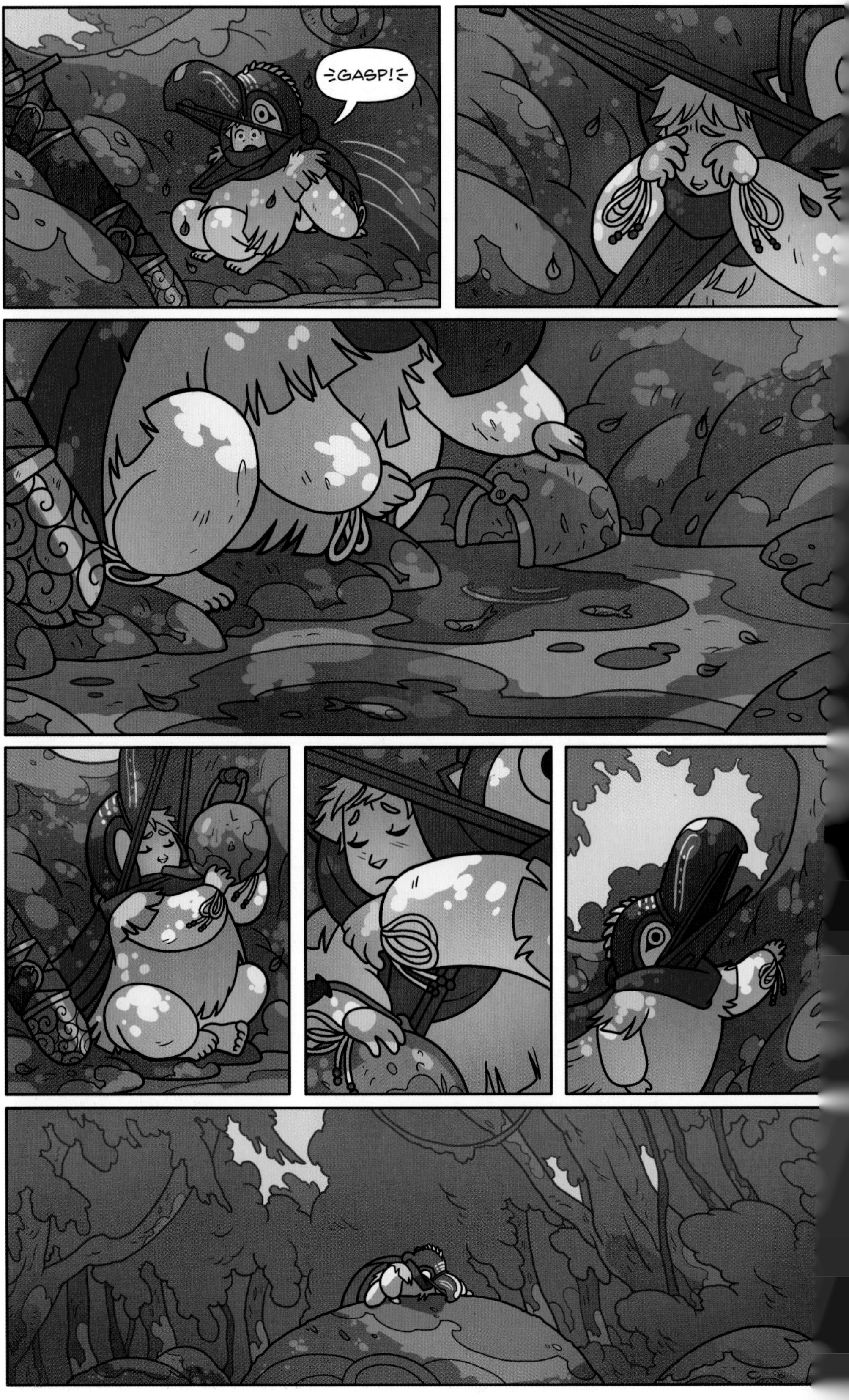
GASP!

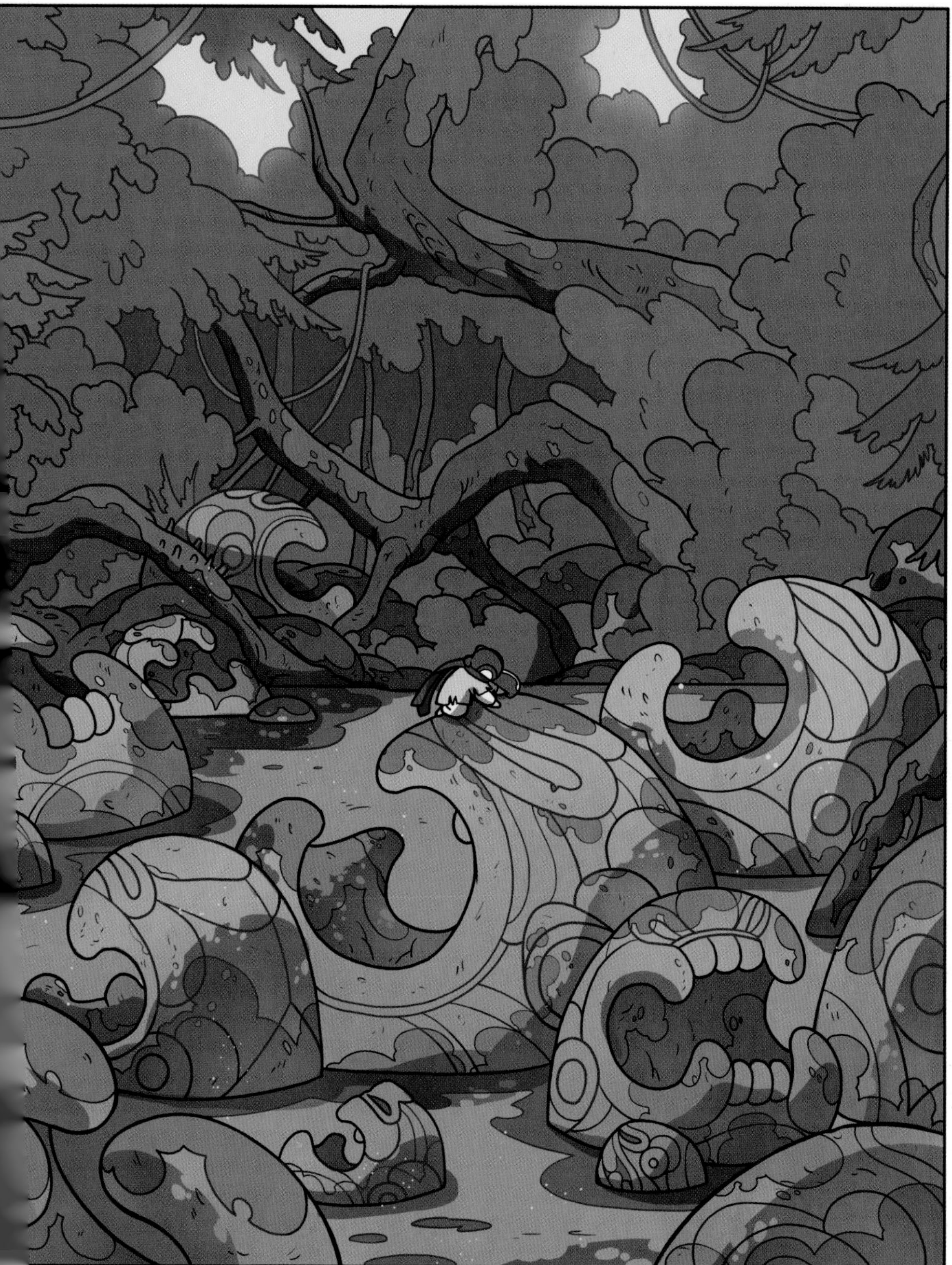

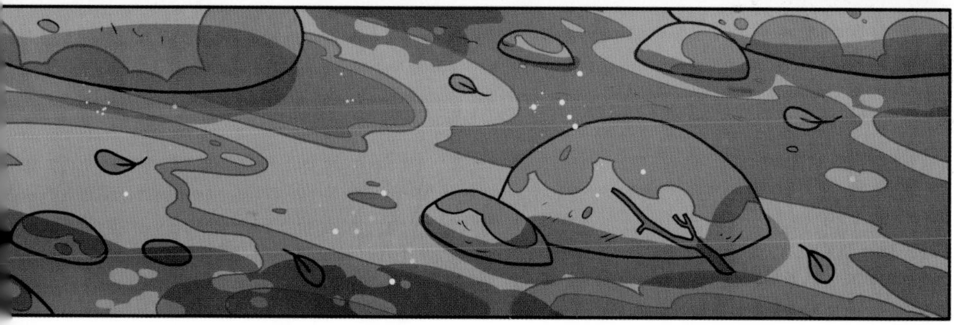

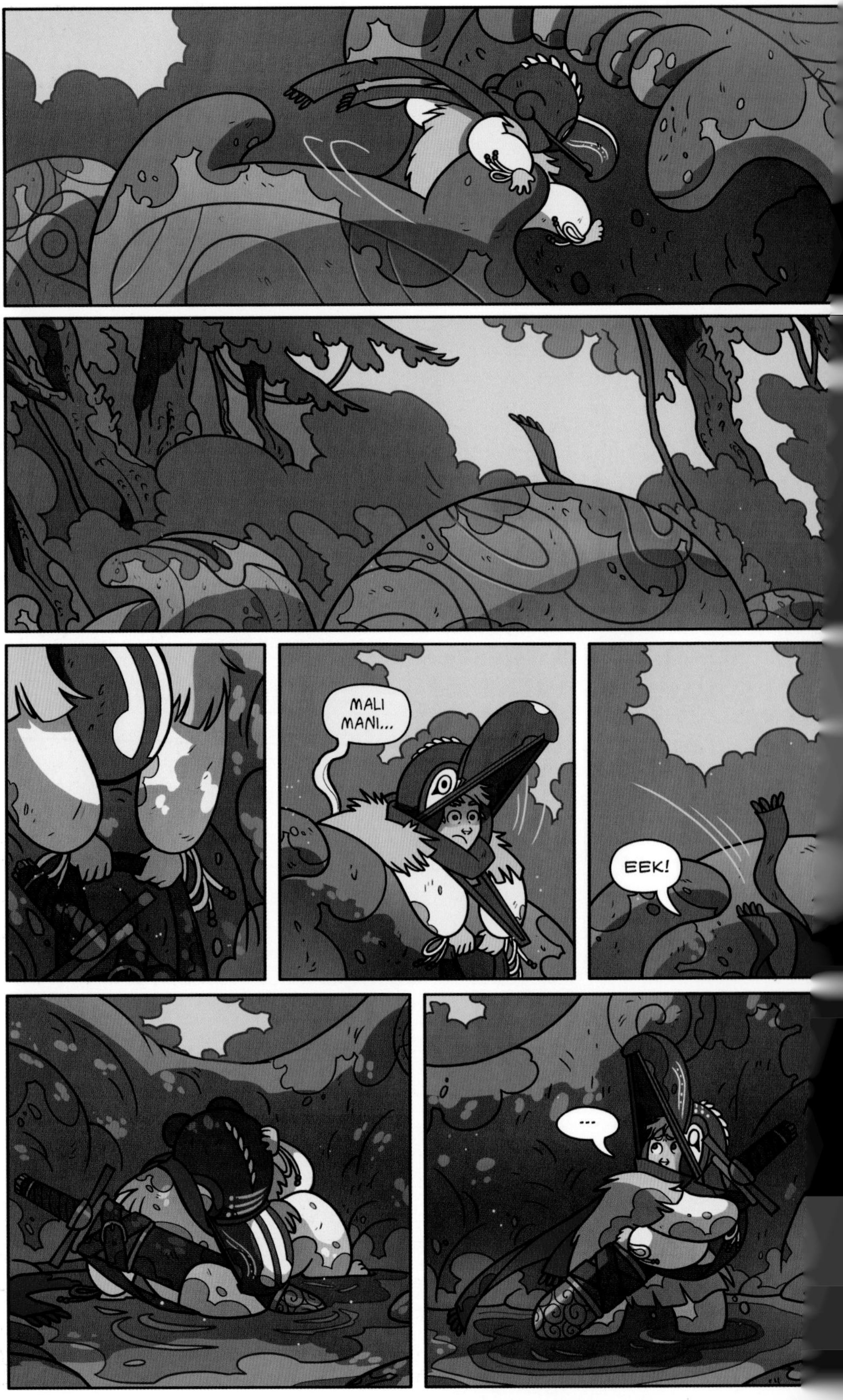
MALI MANI...
EEK!
...

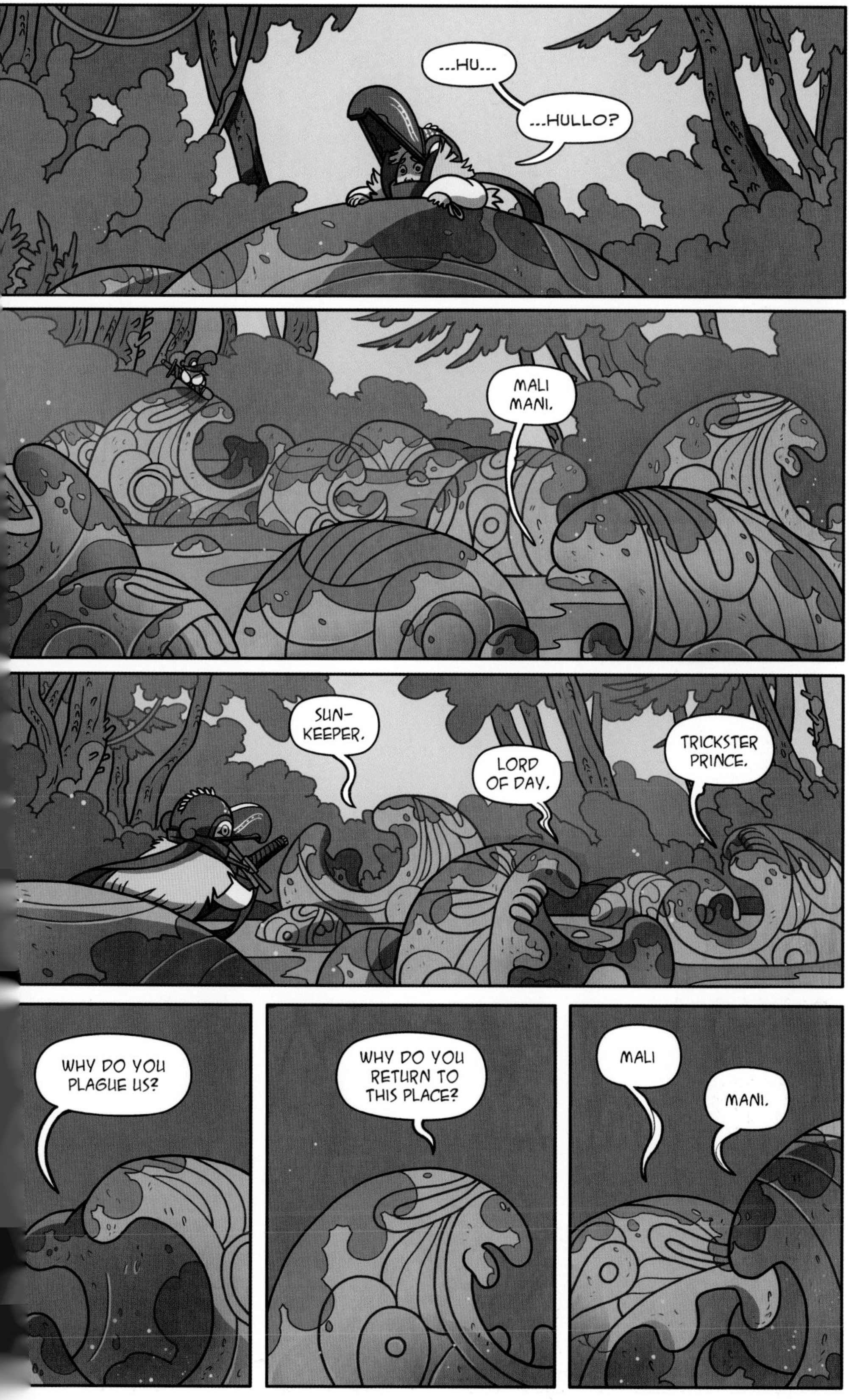
...HU...
...HULLO?
MALI MANI.
SUN-KEEPER.
LORD OF DAY.
TRICKSTER PRINCE.
WHY DO YOU PLAGUE US?
WHY DO YOU RETURN TO THIS PLACE?
MALI
MANI.

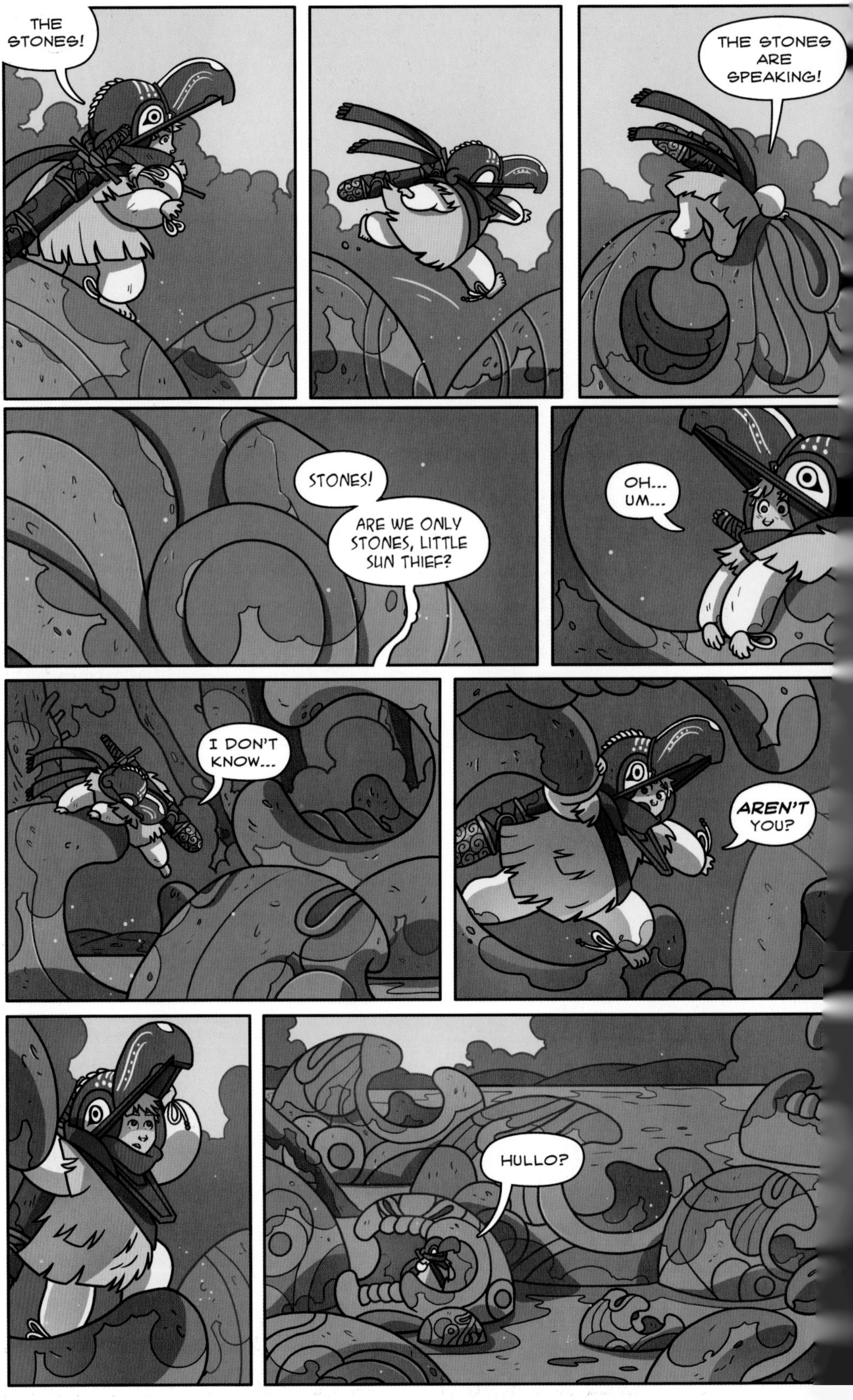
THE STONES!
THE STONES ARE SPEAKING!
STONES!
ARE WE ONLY STONES, LITTLE SUN THIEF?
OH... UM...
I DON'T KNOW...
AREN'T YOU?
HULLO?

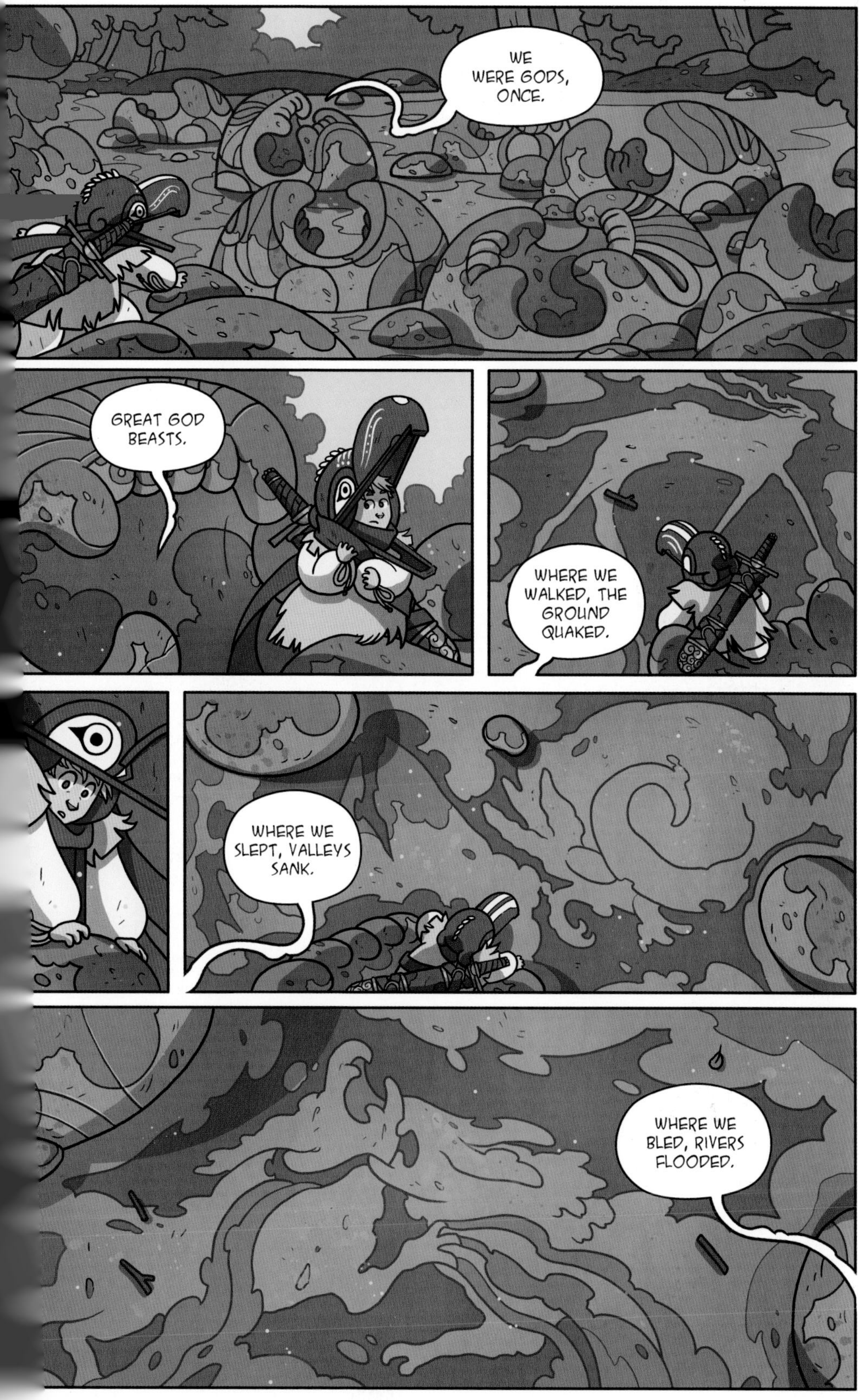
WE WERE GODS, ONCE.
GREAT GOD BEASTS.
WHERE WE WALKED, THE GROUND QUAKED.
WHERE WE SLEPT, VALLEYS SANK.
WHERE WE BLED, RIVERS FLOODED.

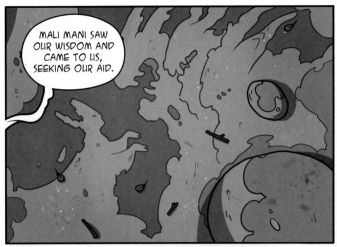

MALI MANI SAW OUR WISDOM AND CAME TO US, SEEKING OUR AID.

WE TAUGHT HIM MANY SECRETS.

MANY TRUTHS.

BUT IT WAS A TRICK.

RUMBLE

AND WE WERE CAST HERE--

--TO FOREVER CURSE HIS NAME!

AH!

MALI MANI!

NOT SO LOUD!

THEY HEAR

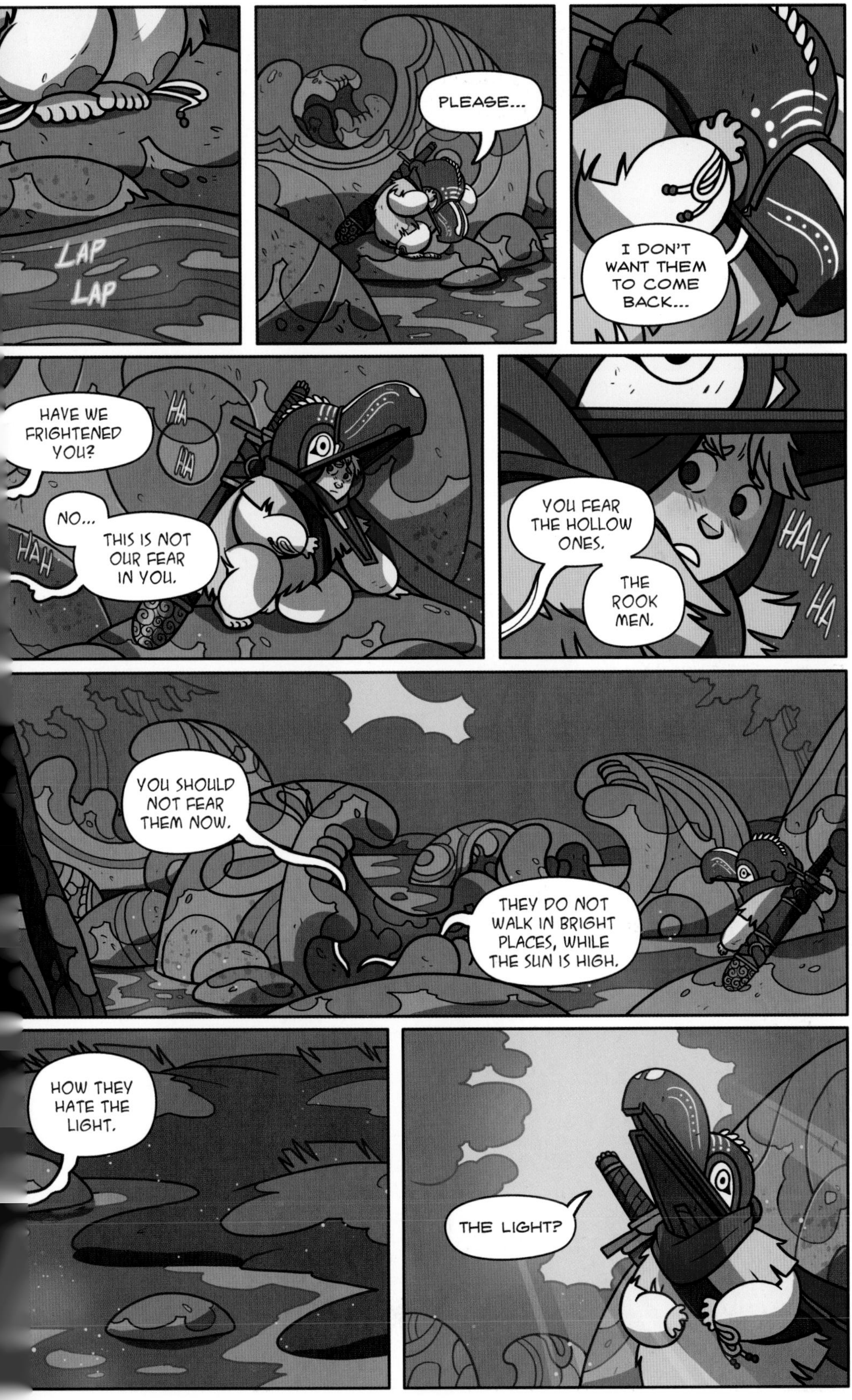
LAP
LAP
PLEASE...
I DON'T WANT THEM TO COME BACK...
HAVE WE FRIGHTENED YOU?
HA
HA
NO...
THIS IS NOT OUR FEAR IN YOU.
HAH
YOU FEAR THE HOLLOW ONES.
THE ROOK MEN.
HAH
HA
YOU SHOULD NOT FEAR THEM NOW.
THEY DO NOT WALK IN BRIGHT PLACES, WHILE THE SUN IS HIGH.
HOW THEY HATE THE LIGHT.
THE LIGHT?

WAIT.
LAST NIGHT...
THE LIGHT... THE FIGURES IN THE SKY...
THE SWORD STOPPED THEM!
BUT...
THEY WERE LOOKING FOR IT, WEREN'T THEY?
WHY WOULD THEY LOOK FOR SOMETHING THAT CAN HURT THEM?

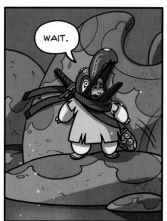

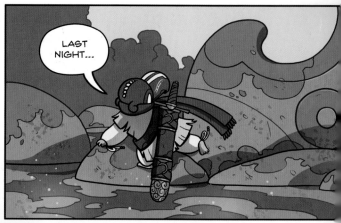

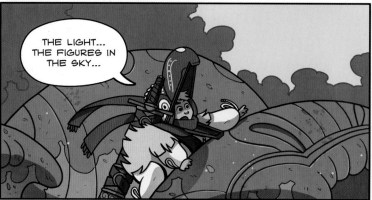

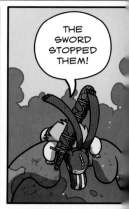

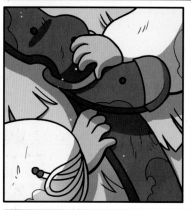

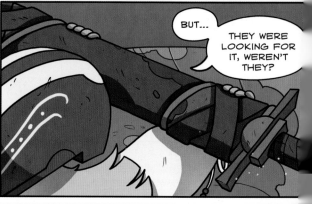

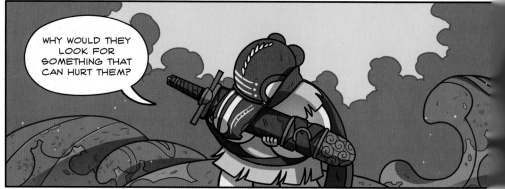

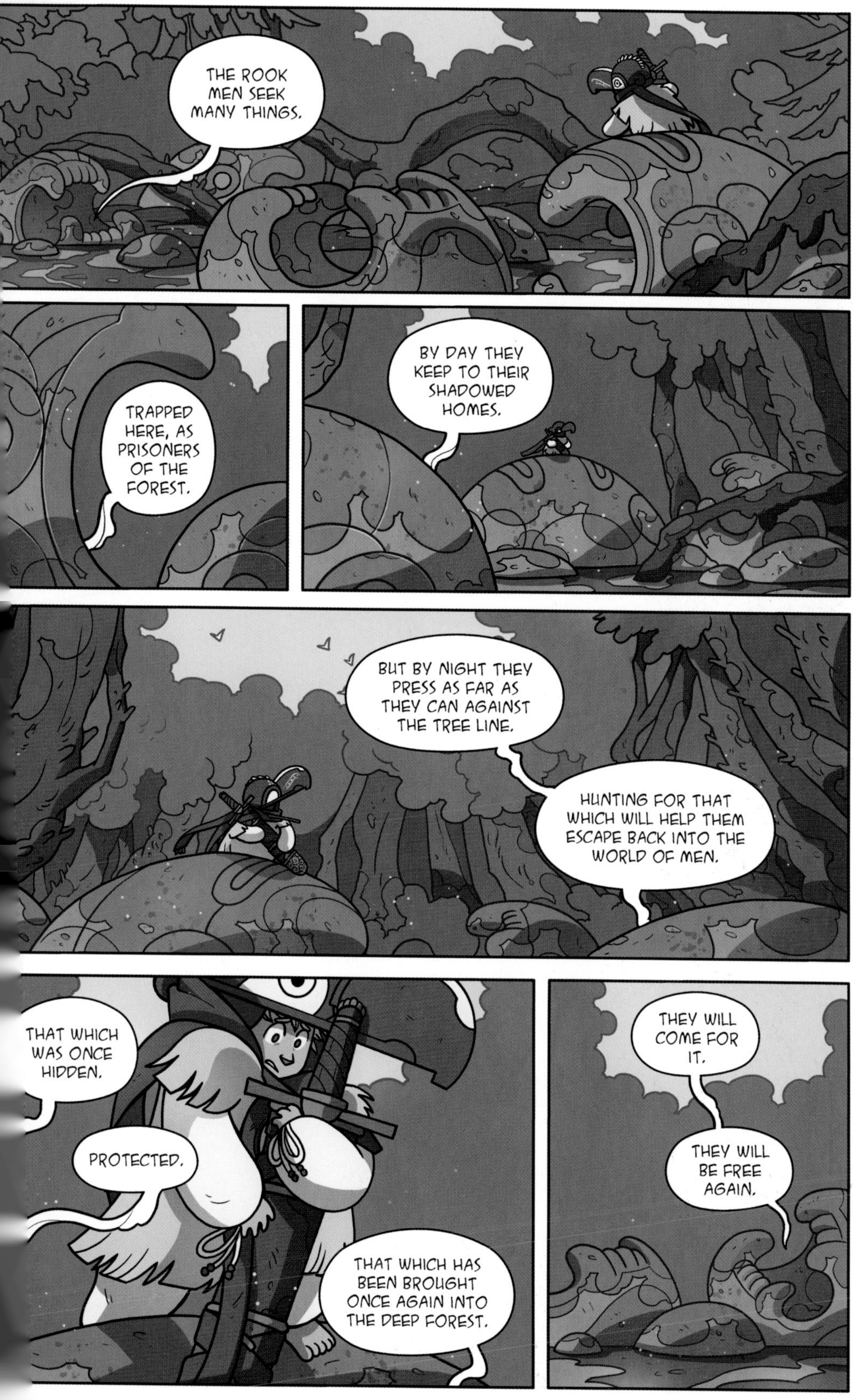
THE ROOK MEN SEEK MANY THINGS.
TRAPPED HERE, AS PRISONERS OF THE FOREST.
BY DAY THEY KEEP TO THEIR SHADOWED HOMES.
BUT BY NIGHT THEY PRESS AS FAR AS THEY CAN AGAINST THE TREE LINE.
HUNTING FOR THAT WHICH WILL HELP THEM ESCAPE BACK INTO THE WORLD OF MEN.
THAT WHICH WAS ONCE HIDDEN.
PROTECTED.
THAT WHICH HAS BEEN BROUGHT ONCE AGAIN INTO THE DEEP FOREST.
THEY WILL COME FOR IT.
THEY WILL BE FREE AGAIN.

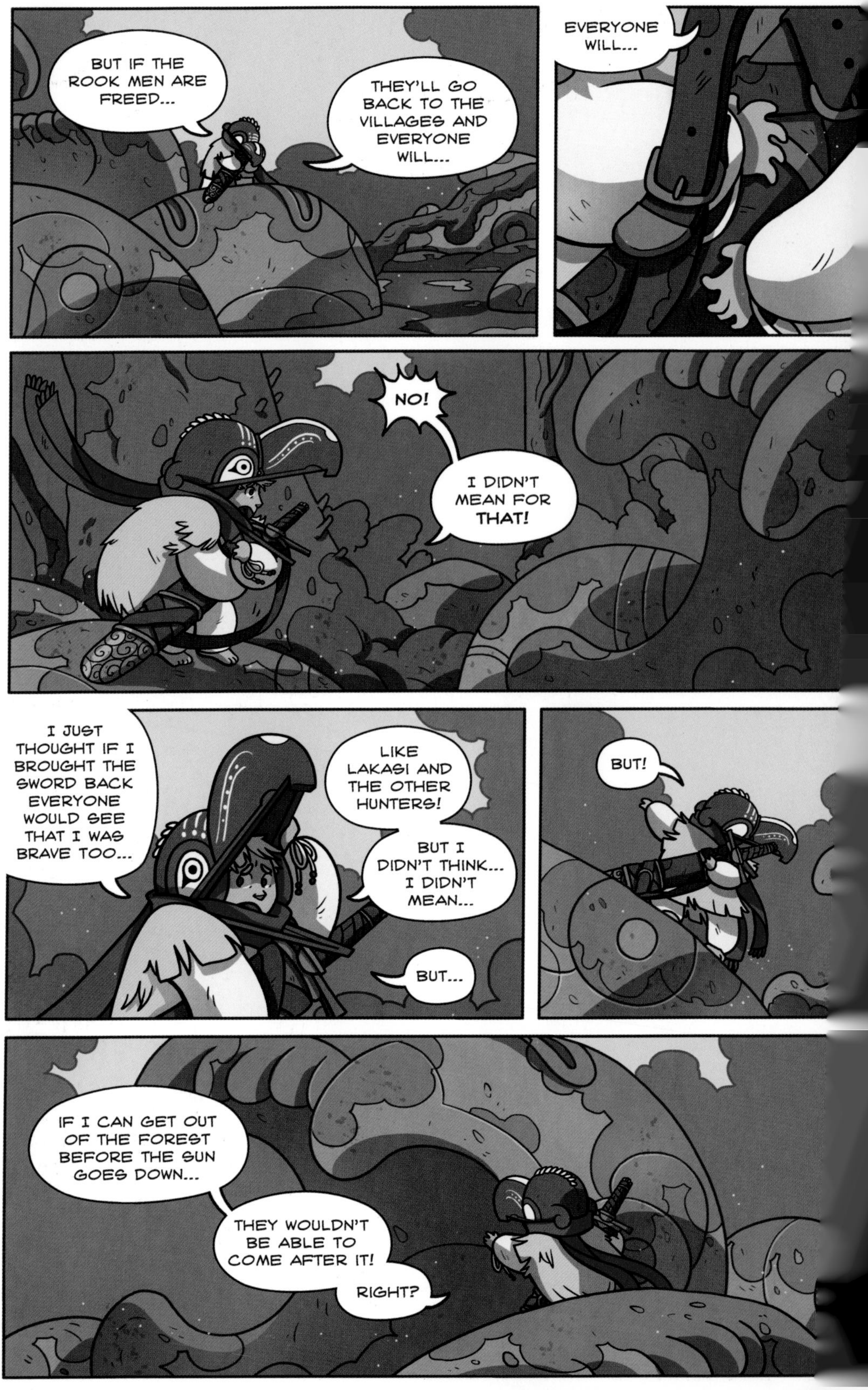
BUT IF THE ROOK MEN ARE FREED...
THEY'LL GO BACK TO THE VILLAGES AND EVERYONE WILL...
EVERYONE WILL...
NO!
I DIDN'T MEAN FOR THAT!
I JUST THOUGHT IF I BROUGHT THE SWORD BACK EVERYONE WOULD SEE THAT I WAS BRAVE TOO...
LIKE LAKASI AND THE OTHER HUNTERS!
BUT I DIDN'T THINK... I DIDN'T MEAN...
BUT...
BUT!
IF I CAN GET OUT OF THE FOREST BEFORE THE SUN GOES DOWN...
THEY WOULDN'T BE ABLE TO COME AFTER IT!
RIGHT?

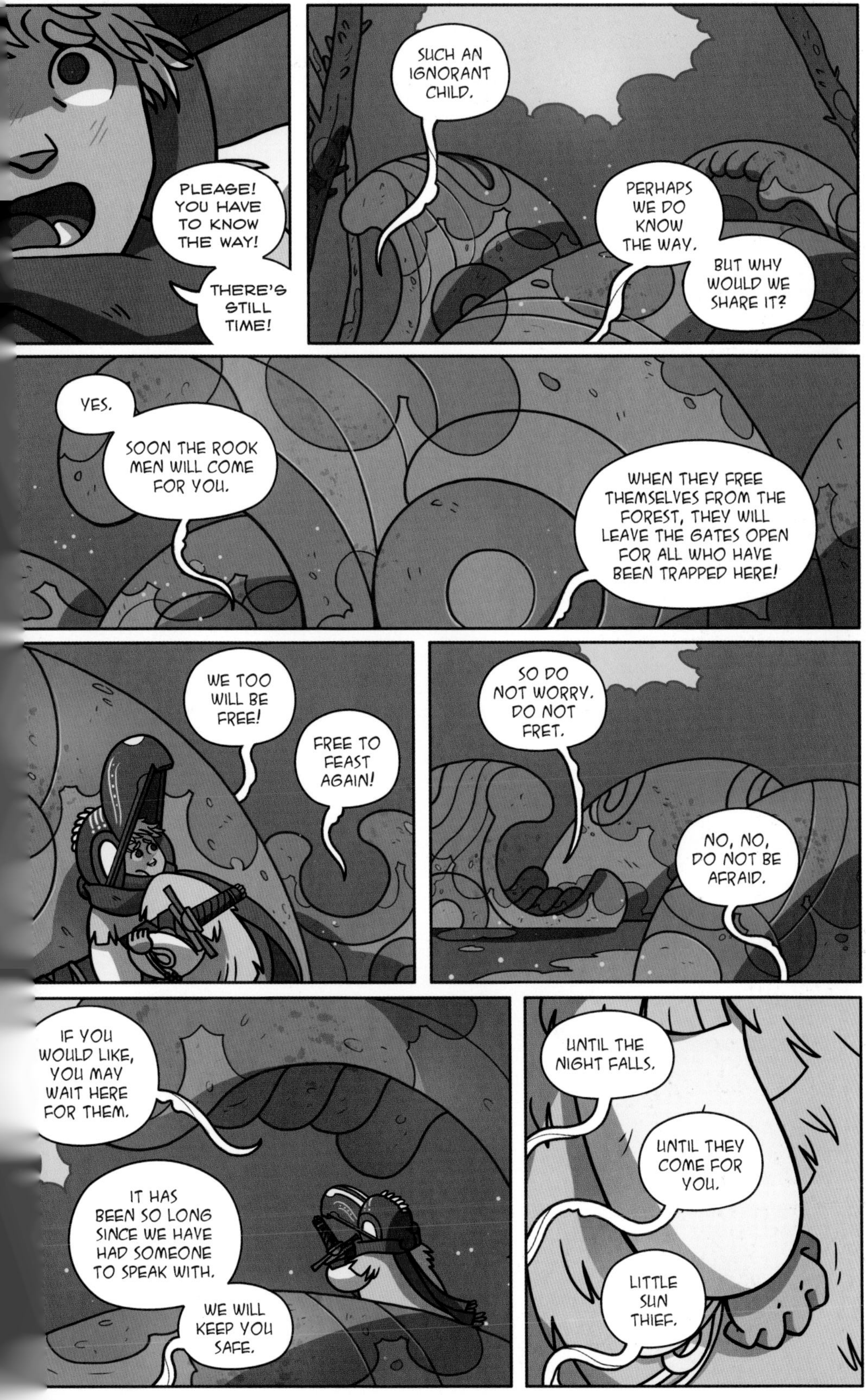
PLEASE! YOU HAVE TO KNOW THE WAY!
THERE'S STILL TIME!
SUCH AN IGNORANT CHILD.
PERHAPS WE DO KNOW THE WAY.
BUT WHY WOULD WE SHARE IT?
YES.
SOON THE ROOK MEN WILL COME FOR YOU.
WHEN THEY FREE THEMSELVES FROM THE FOREST, THEY WILL LEAVE THE GATES OPEN FOR ALL WHO HAVE BEEN TRAPPED HERE!
WE TOO WILL BE FREE!
FREE TO FEAST AGAIN!
SO DO NOT WORRY. DO NOT FRET.
NO, NO, DO NOT BE AFRAID.
IF YOU WOULD LIKE, YOU MAY WAIT HERE FOR THEM.
IT HAS BEEN SO LONG SINCE WE HAVE HAD SOMEONE TO SPEAK WITH.
WE WILL KEEP YOU SAFE.
UNTIL THE NIGHT FALLS.
UNTIL THEY COME FOR YOU.
LITTLE SUN THIEF.

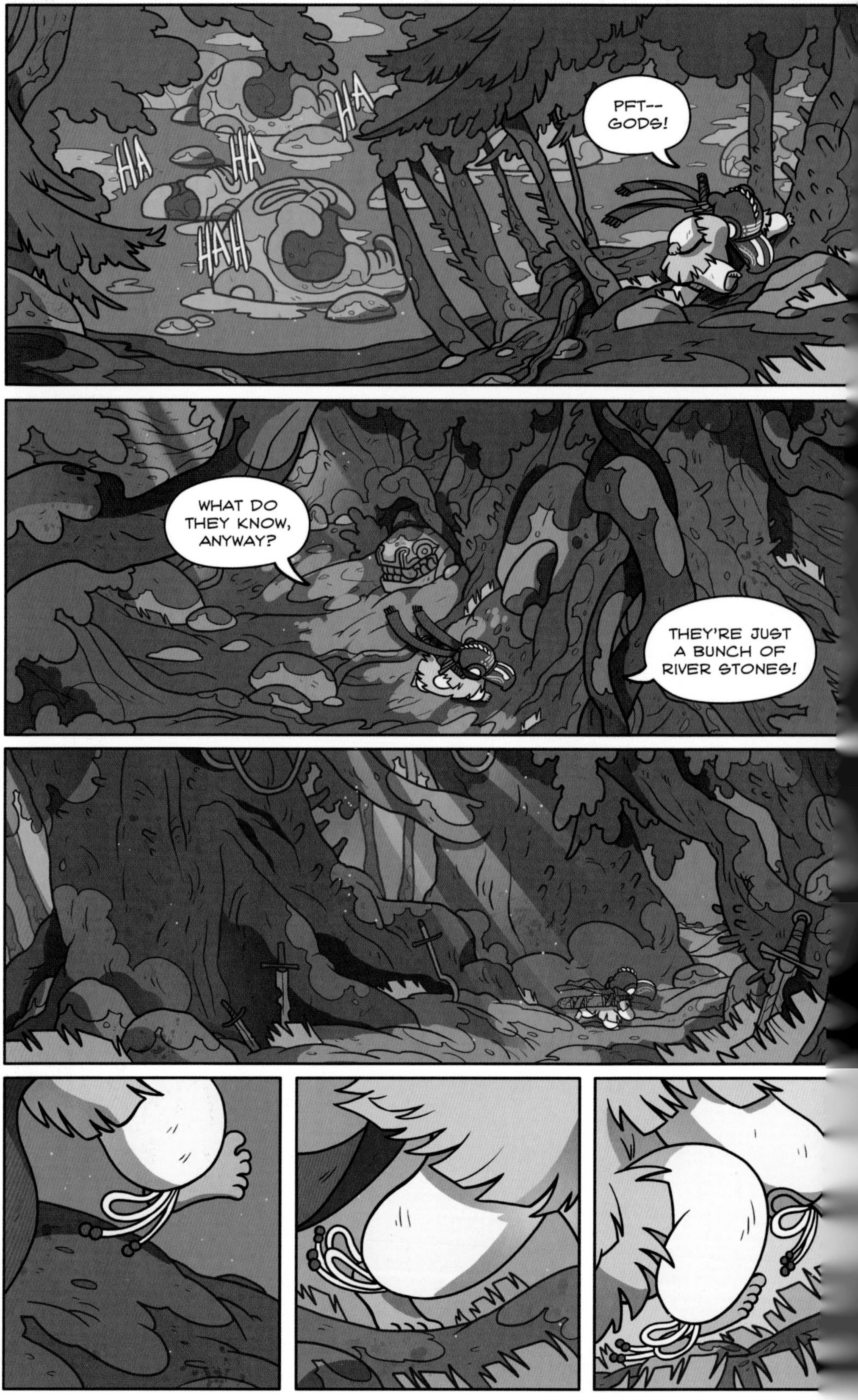
HA
HA
HAH
HA
PFT-- GODS!
WHAT DO THEY KNOW, ANYWAY?
THEY'RE JUST A BUNCH OF RIVER STONES!

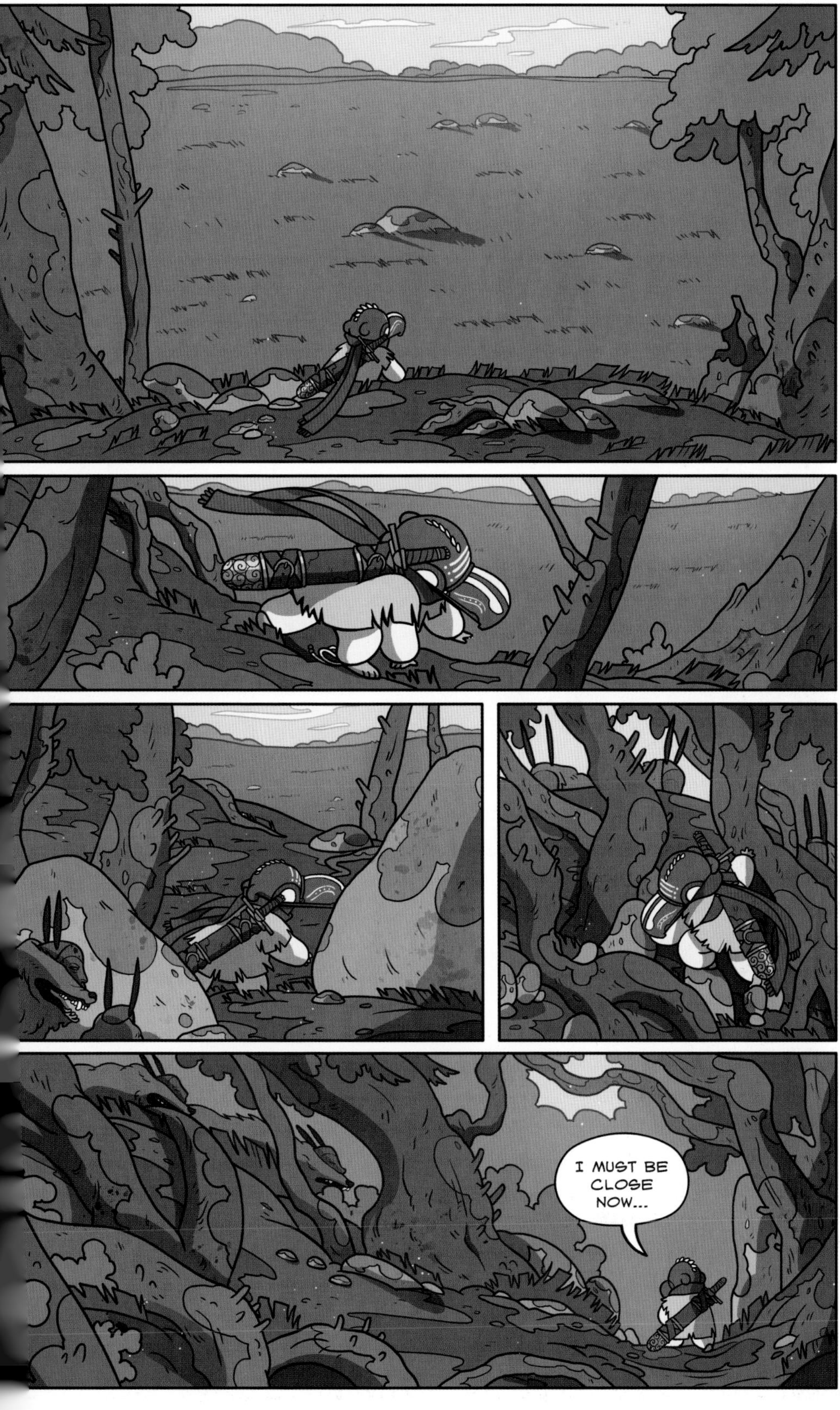
I MUST BE CLOSE NOW...

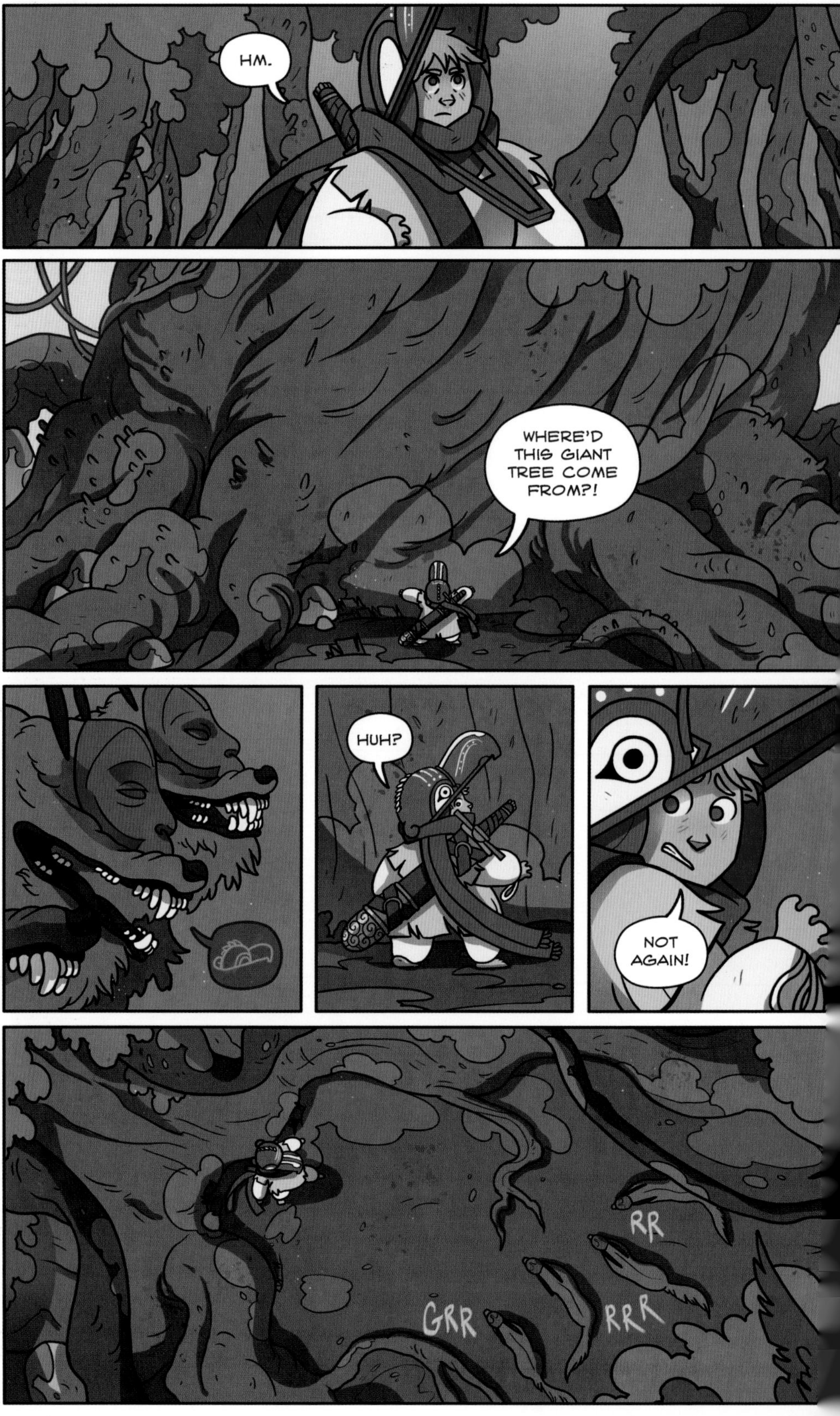
HM.
WHERE'D THIS GIANT TREE COME FROM?!
HUH?
NOT AGAIN!
GRR
RRR
RR

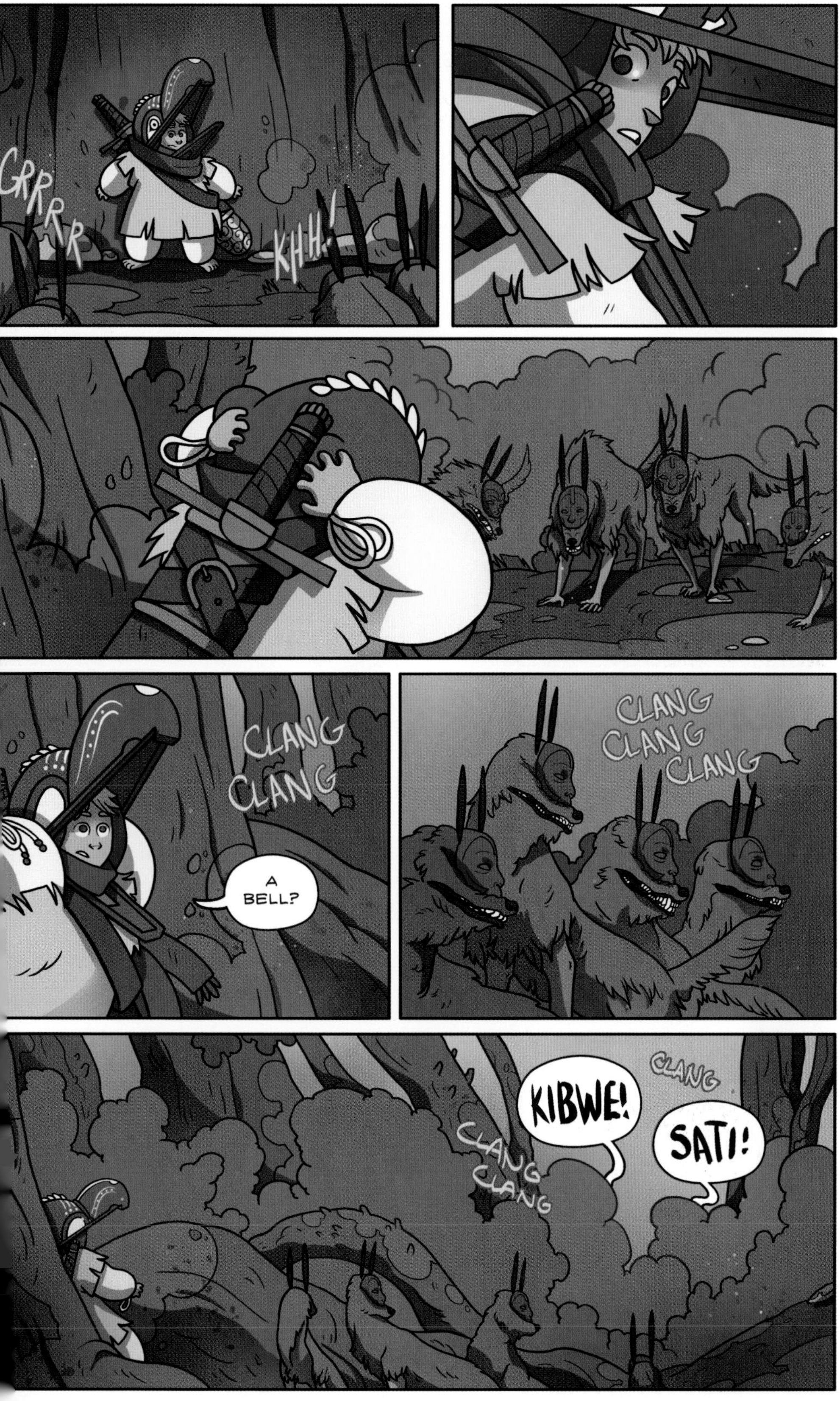
GRRRRR
KHH!
CLANG
CLANG
A BELL?
CLANG
CLANG
CLANG
KIBWE!
SATI!
CLANG
CLANG
CLANG

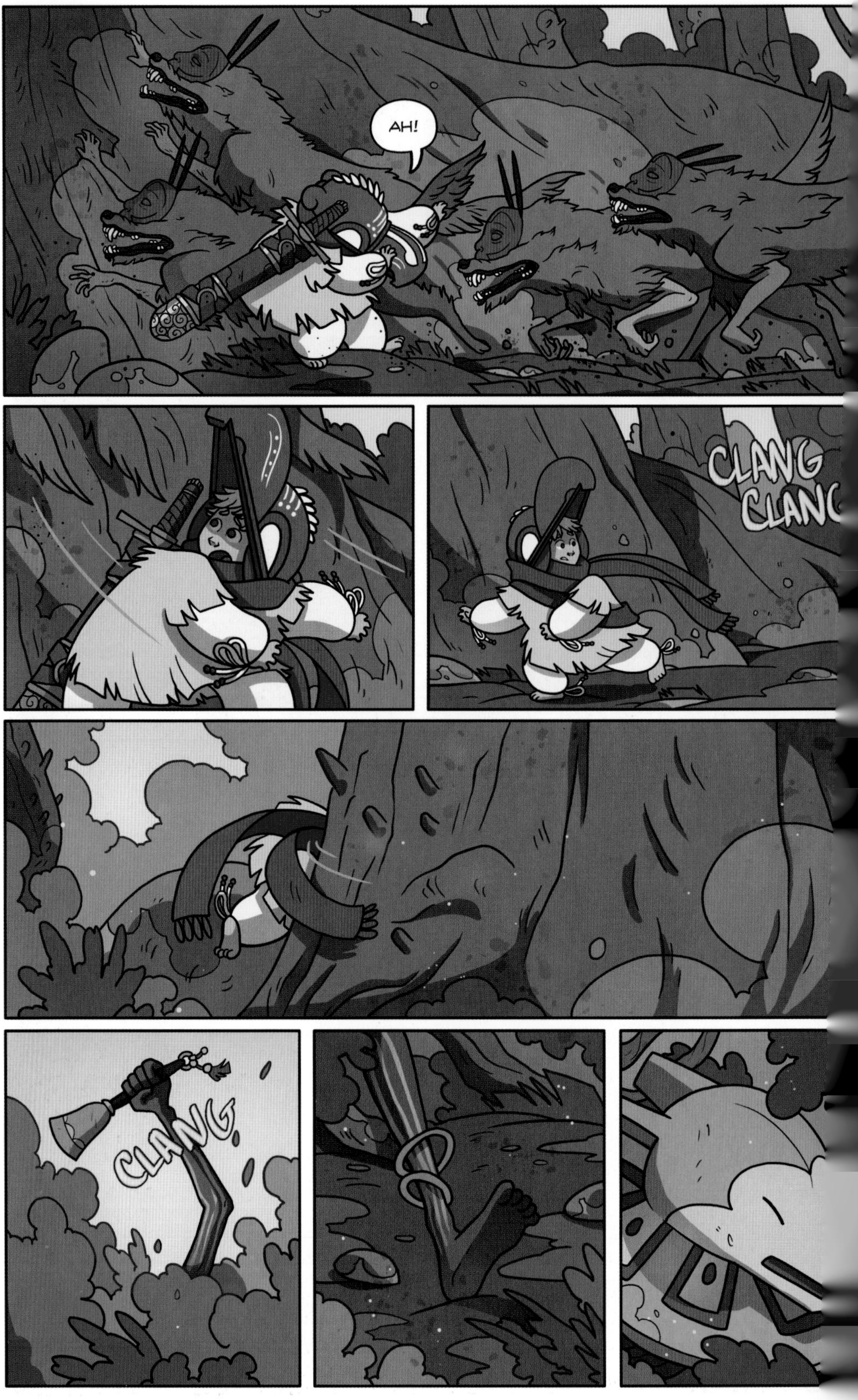
AH!
CLANG
CLANG
CLANG

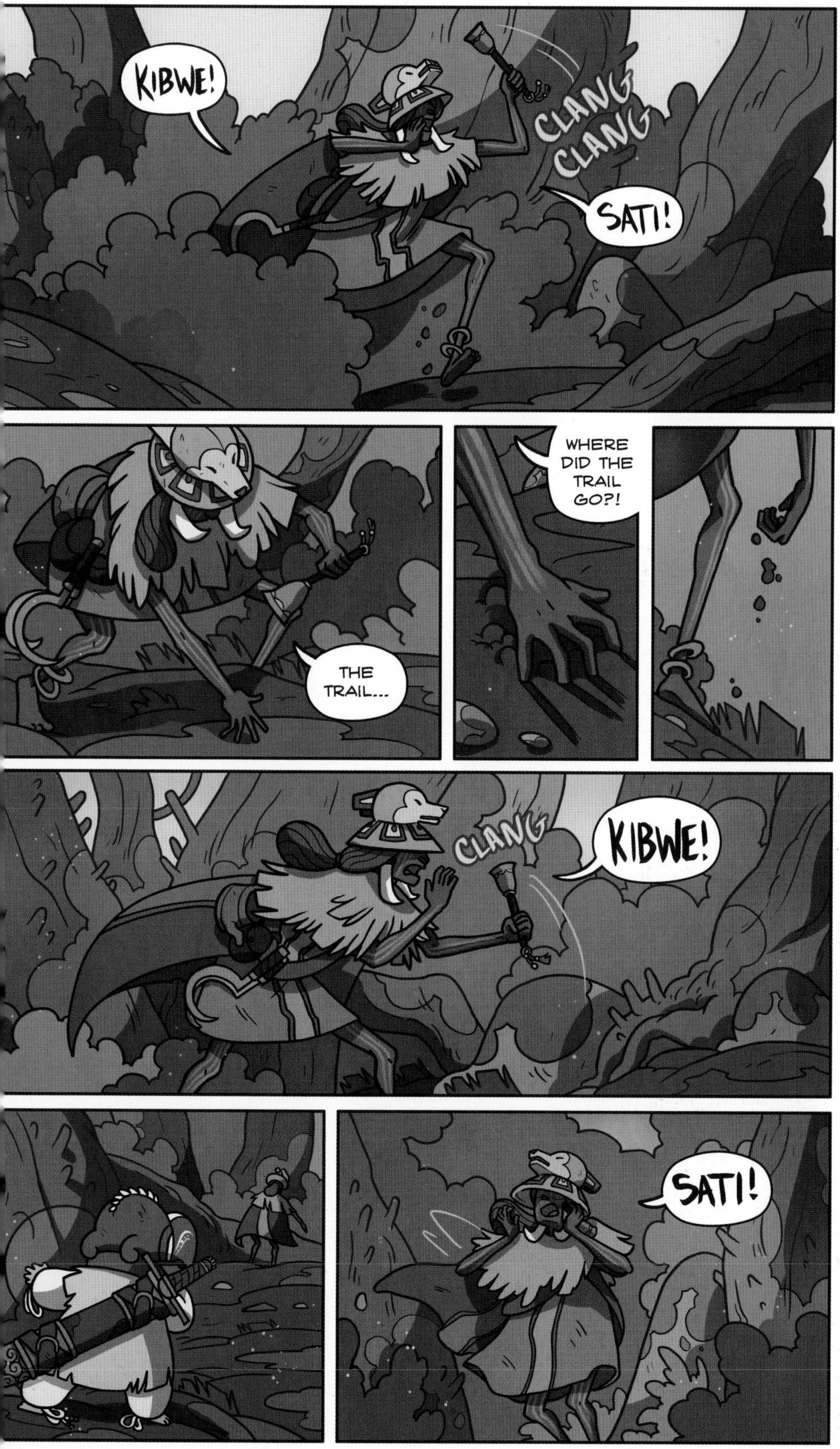
KIBWE!
CLANG
CLANG
SATI!
THE TRAIL...
WHERE DID THE TRAIL GO?!
CLANG
KIBWE!
SATI!

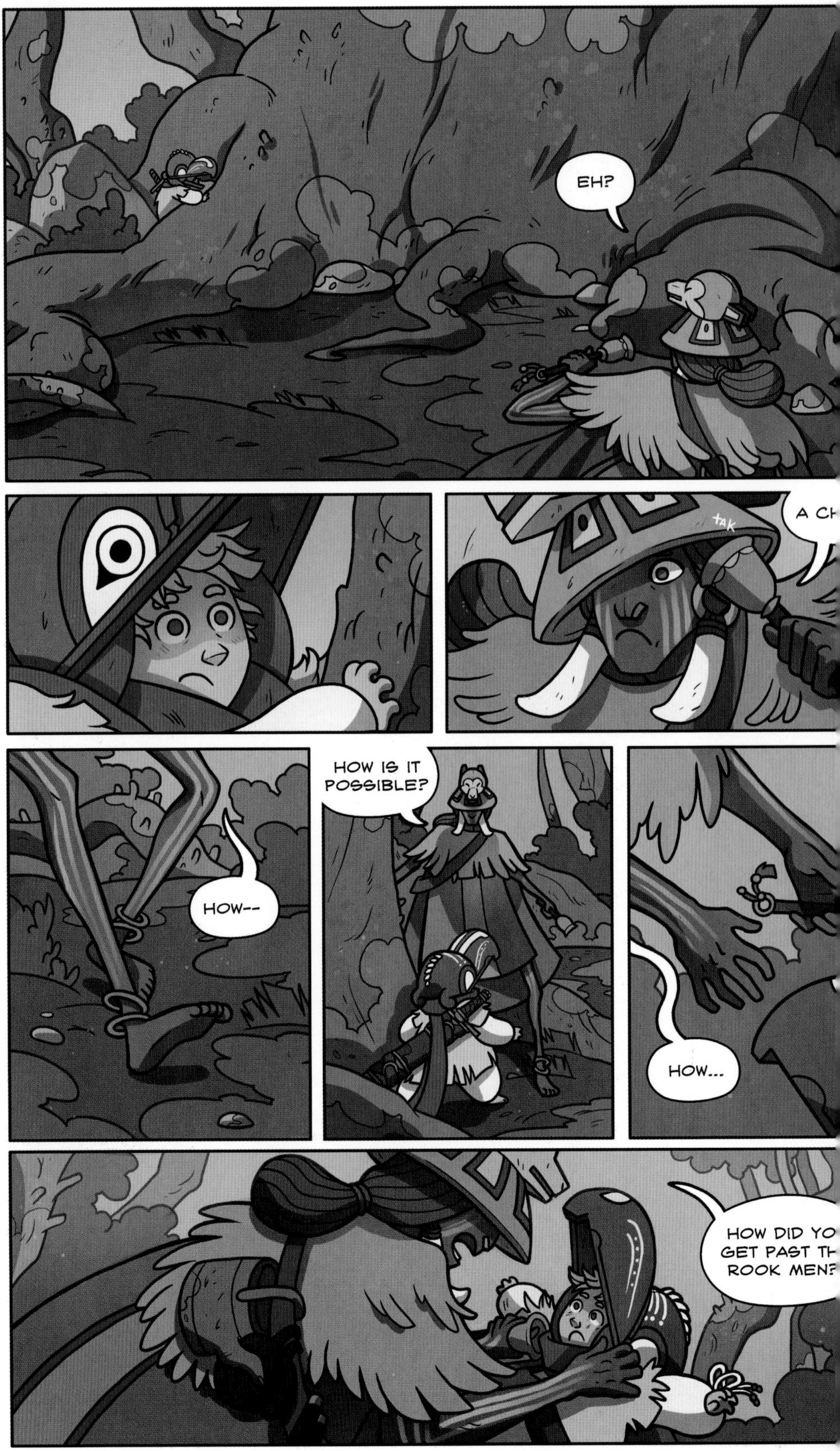
EH?
A CH
TAK
HOW--
HOW IS IT POSSIBLE?
HOW...
HOW DID YO
GET PAST TH
ROOK MEN?

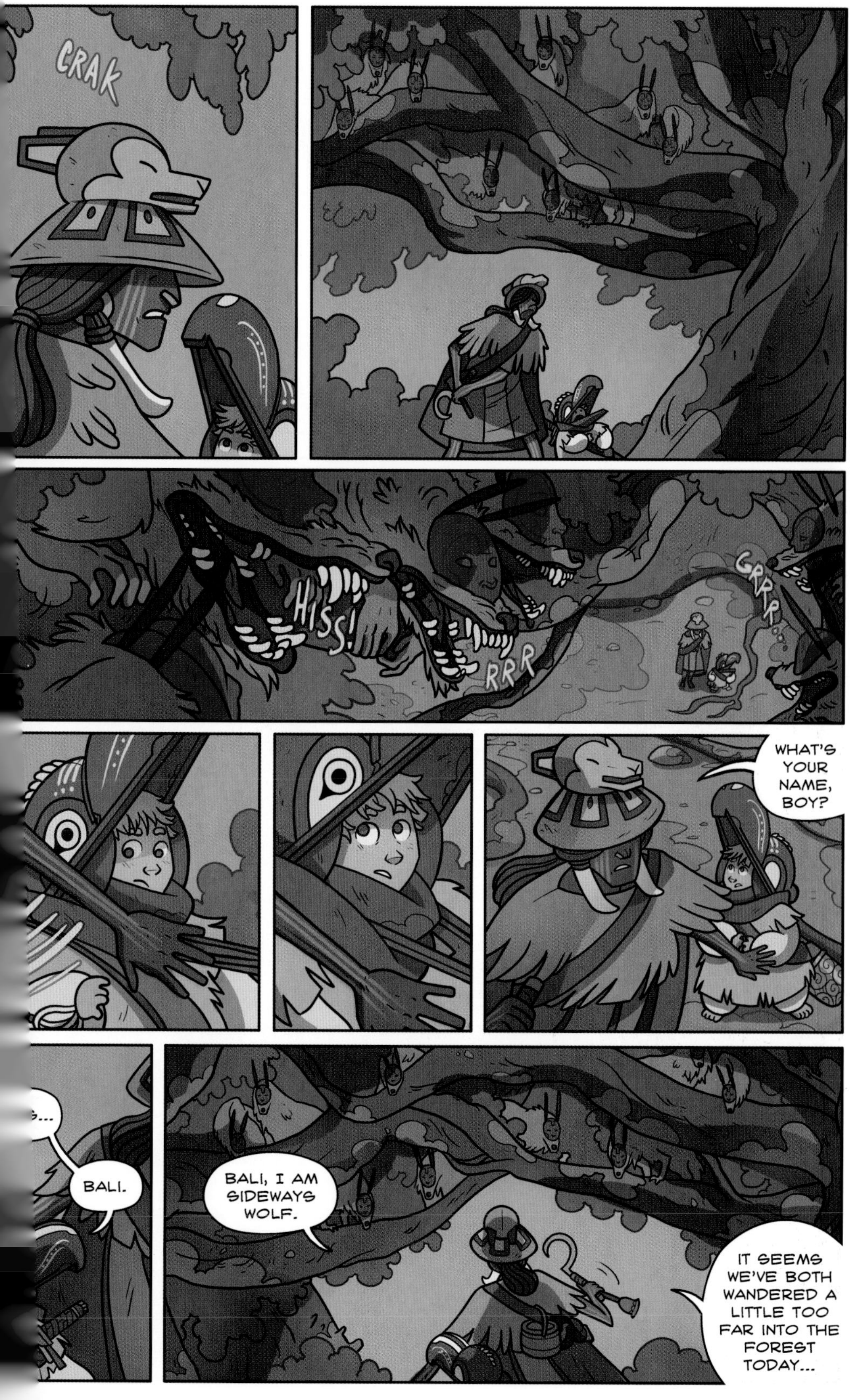
CRAK
HISS!
RRR
GRRRR
WHAT'S YOUR NAME, BOY?
BALI.
BALI, I AM SIDEWAYS WOLF.
IT SEEMS WE'VE BOTH WANDERED A LITTLE TOO FAR INTO THE FOREST TODAY...

ARE YOU READY TO RUN?

KRR KRR HISS!

SNATCH

LET'S GO!

SNAP

SWIPE

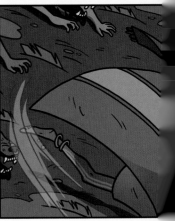

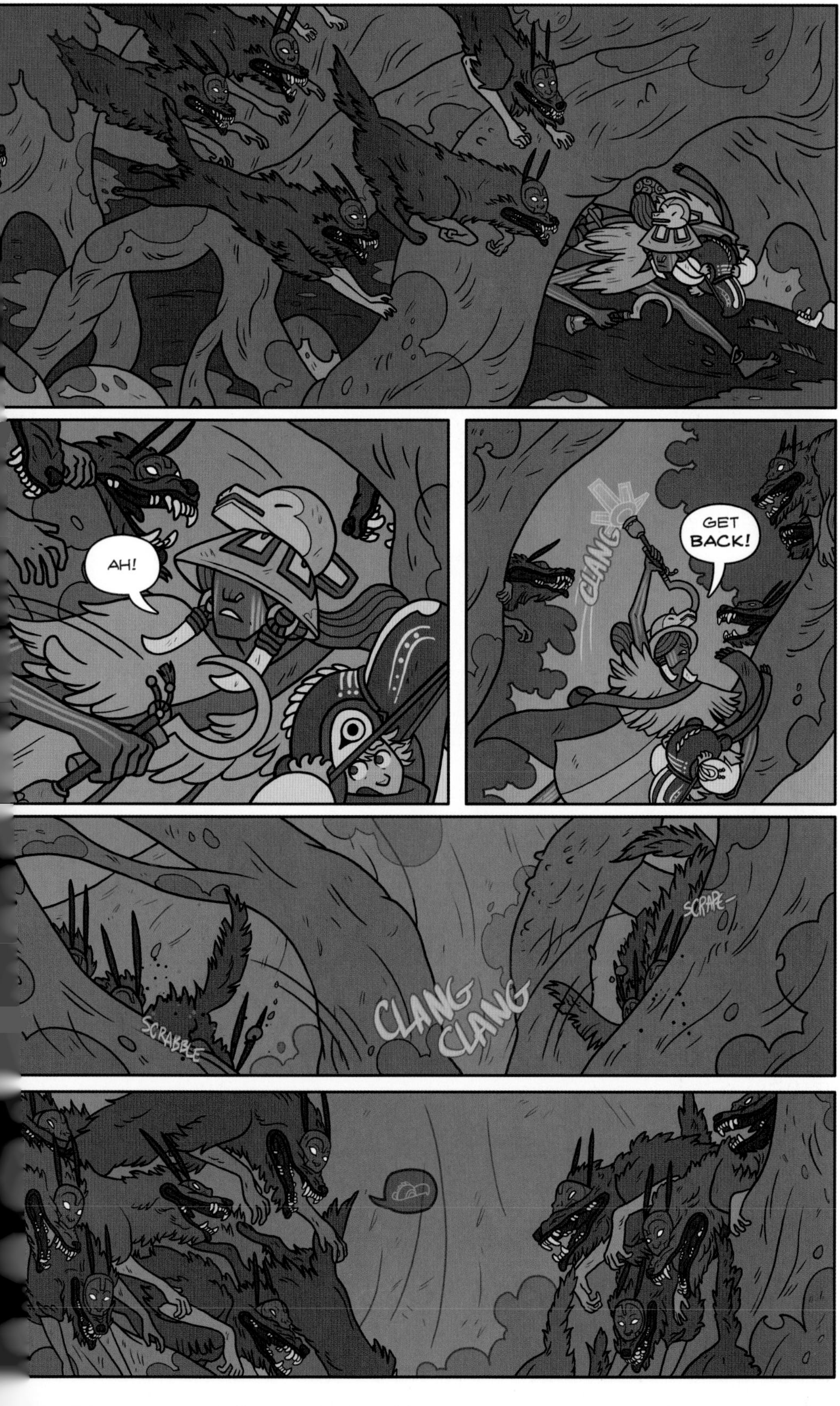
AH!
CLANG
GET BACK!
SCRAPE-
SCRABBLE
CLANG CLANG

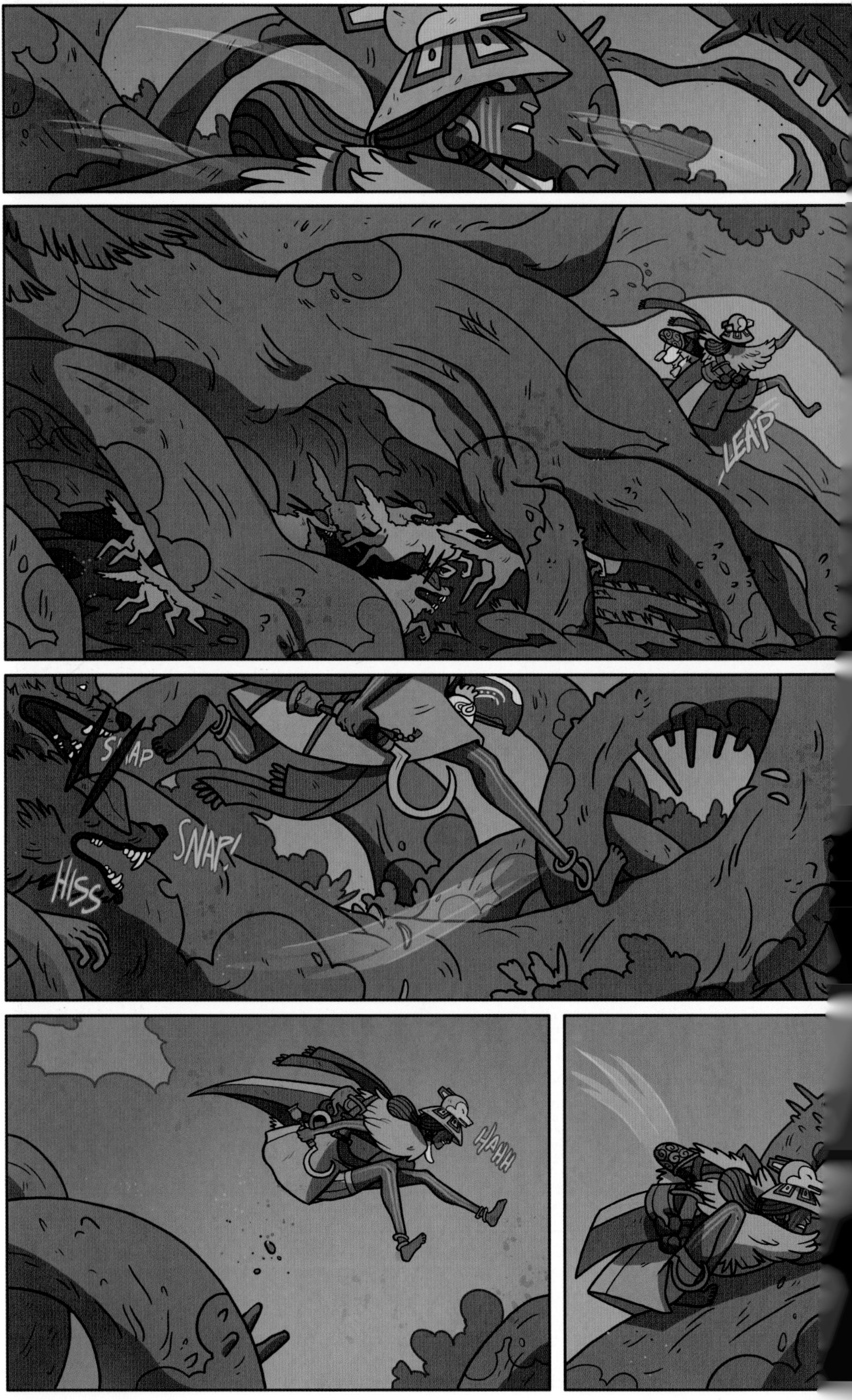
LEAP
SNAP
SNAP!
HISS
HAHH

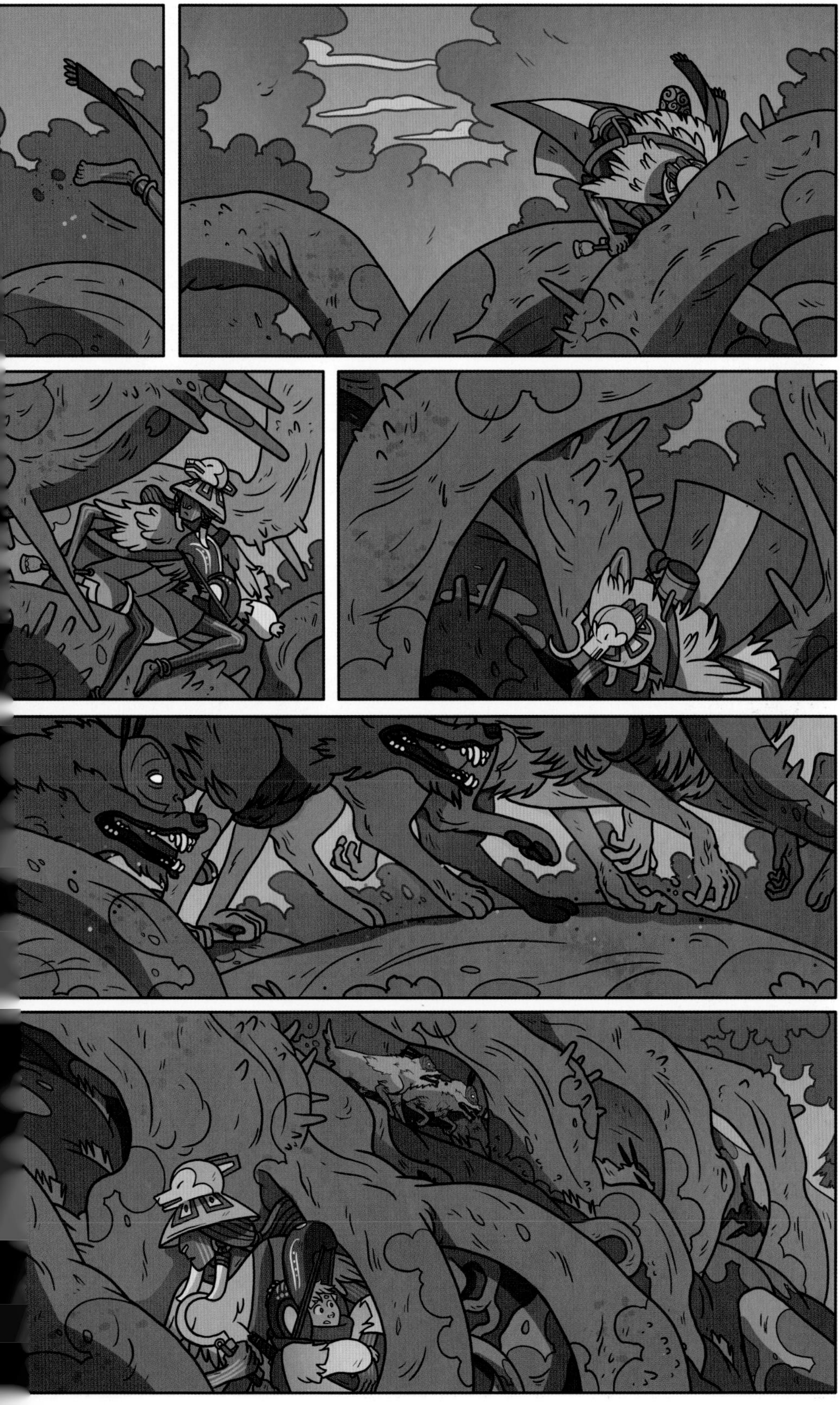

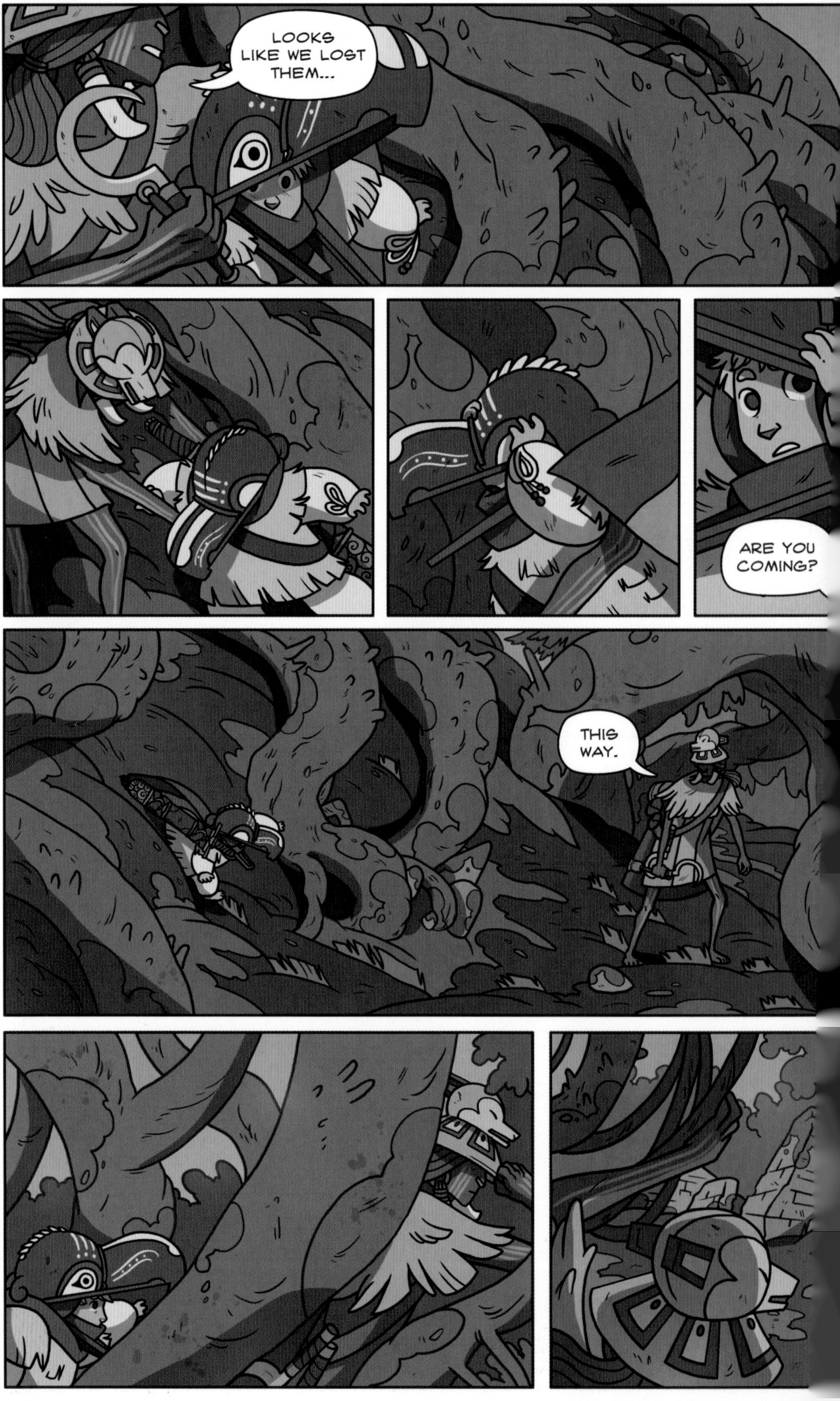
LOOKS LIKE WE LOST THEM...
ARE YOU COMING?
THIS WAY.

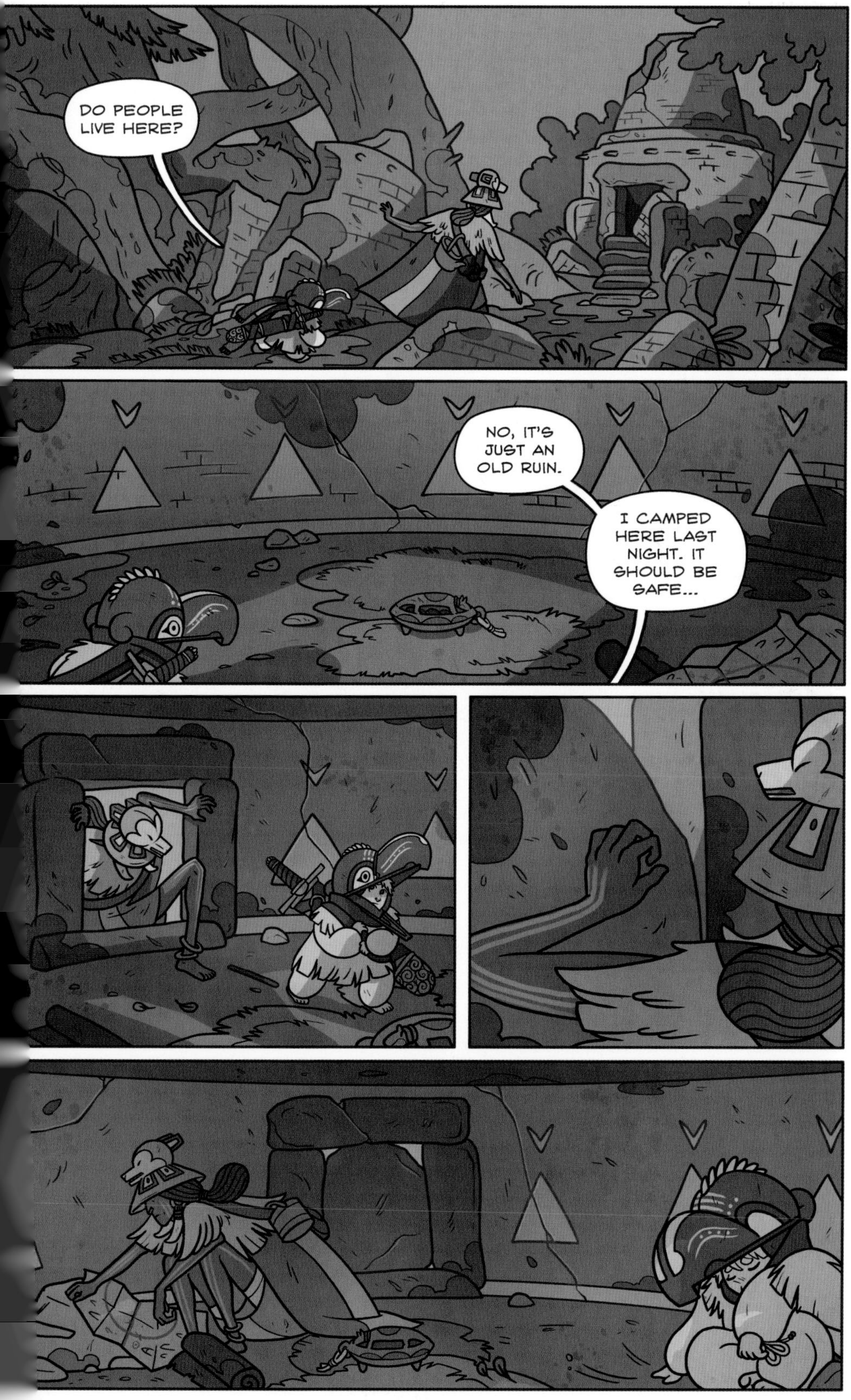
DO PEOPLE LIVE HERE?
NO, IT'S JUST AN OLD RUIN.
I CAMPED HERE LAST NIGHT. IT SHOULD BE SAFE...

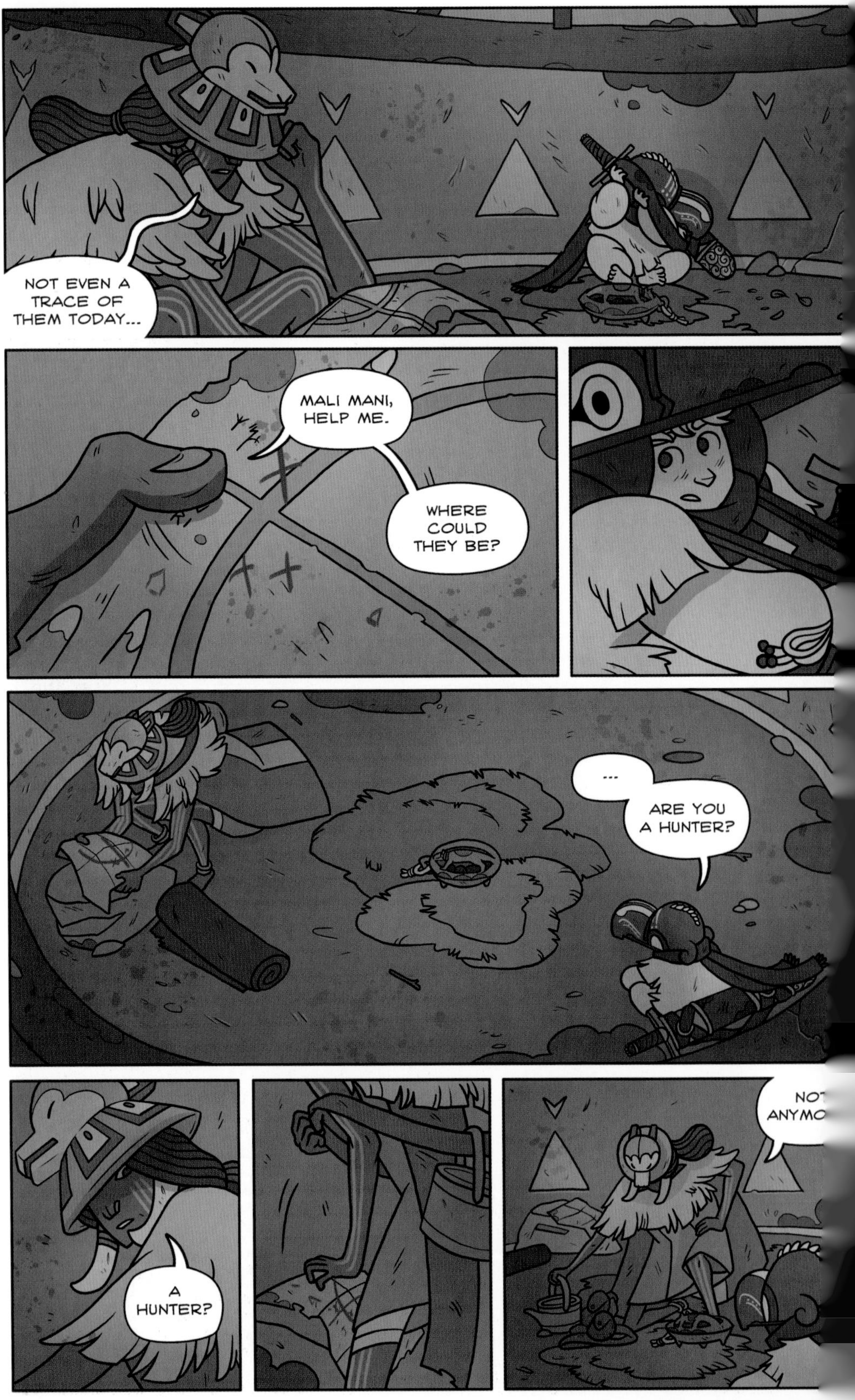
NOT EVEN A TRACE OF THEM TODAY...
MALI MANI, HELP ME.
WHERE COULD THEY BE?
...
ARE YOU A HUNTER?
A HUNTER?

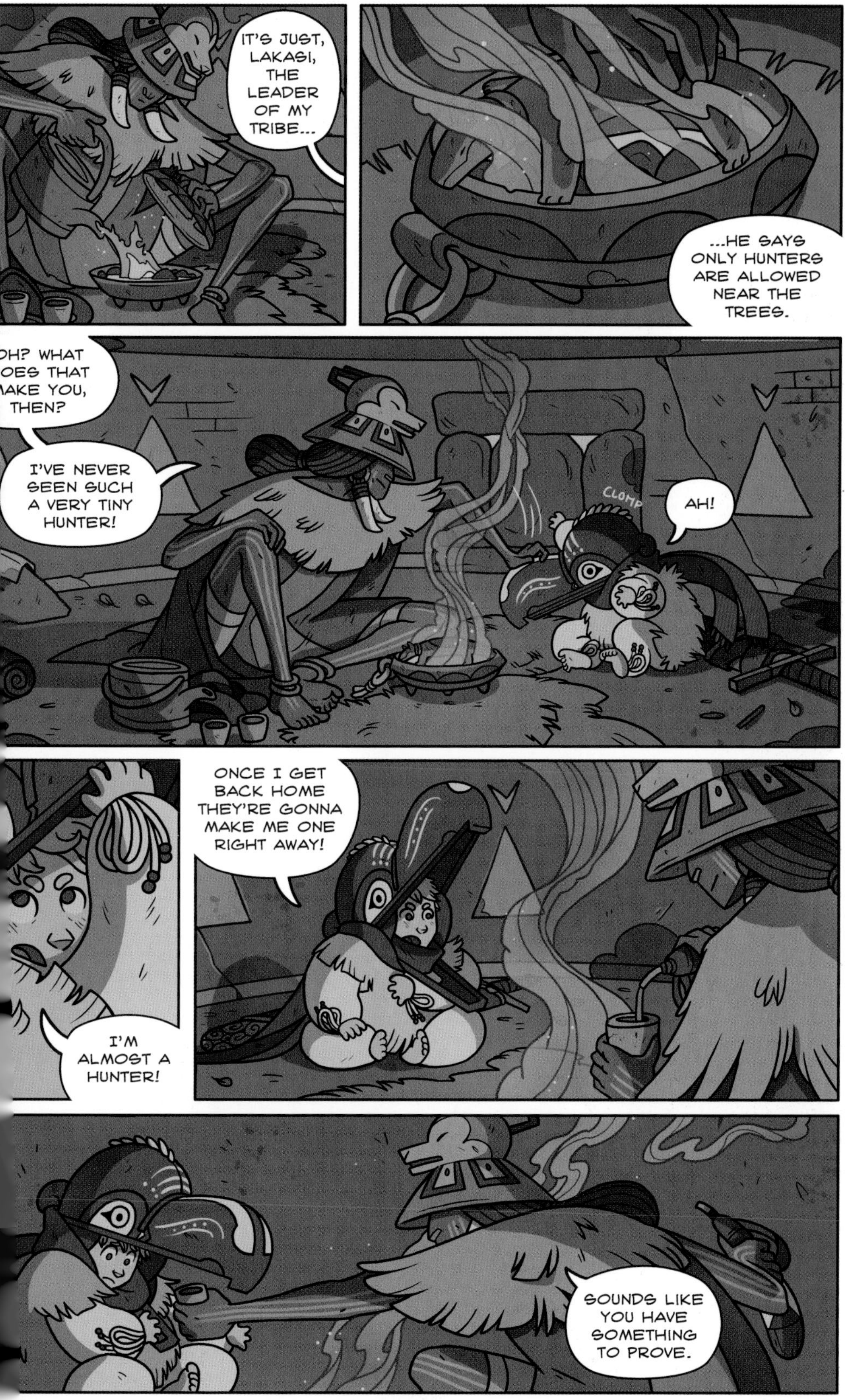

IT'S JUST, LAKASI, THE LEADER OF MY TRIBE...
...HE SAYS ONLY HUNTERS ARE ALLOWED NEAR THE TREES.
OH? WHAT DOES THAT MAKE YOU, THEN?
I'VE NEVER SEEN SUCH A VERY TINY HUNTER!
CLOMP
AH!
I'M ALMOST A HUNTER!
ONCE I GET BACK HOME THEY'RE GONNA MAKE ME ONE RIGHT AWAY!
SOUNDS LIKE YOU HAVE SOMETHING TO PROVE.

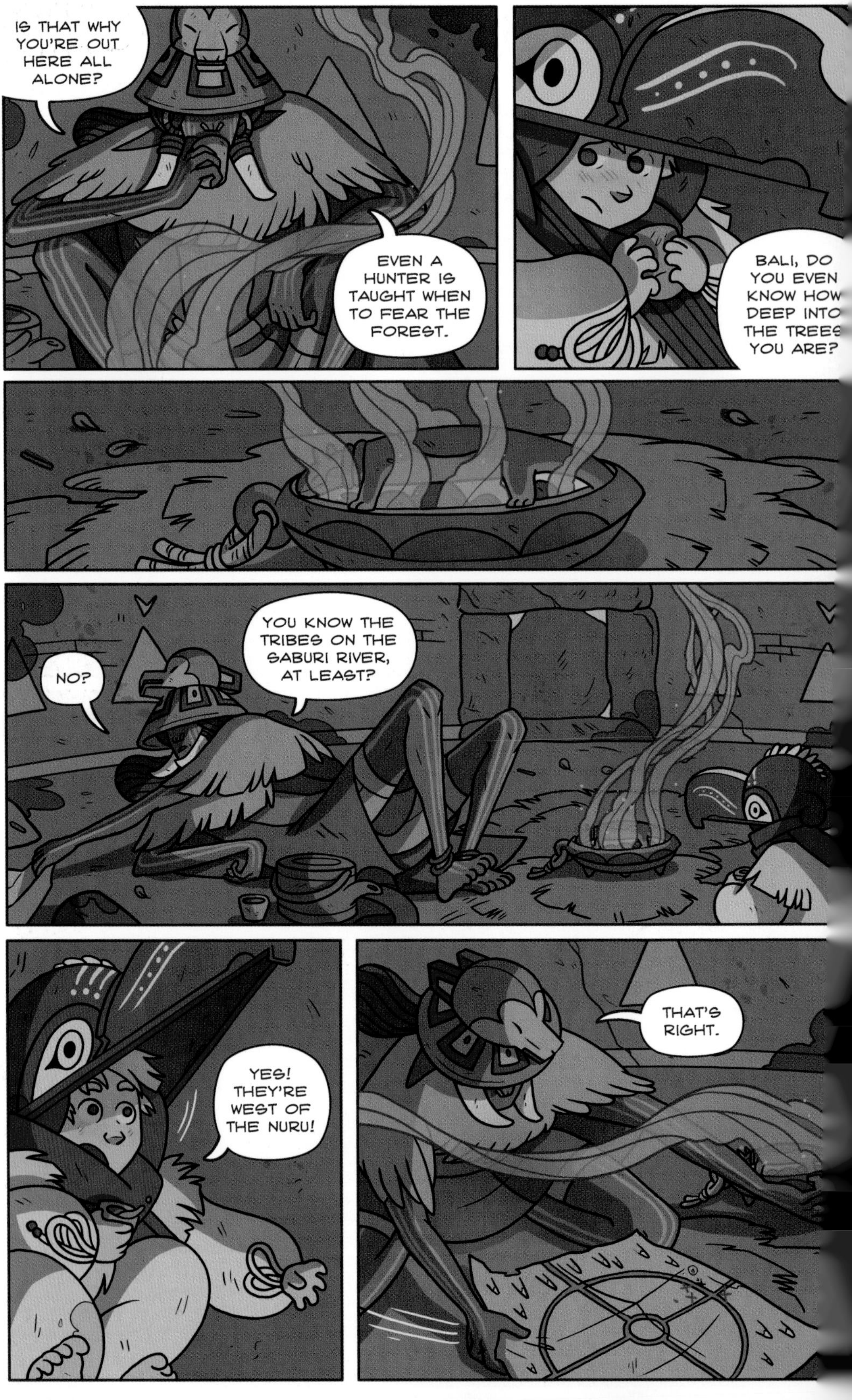
IS THAT WHY YOU'RE OUT HERE ALL ALONE?
EVEN A HUNTER IS TAUGHT WHEN TO FEAR THE FOREST.
BALI, DO YOU EVEN KNOW HOW DEEP INTO THE TREES YOU ARE?
NO?
YOU KNOW THE TRIBES ON THE SABURI RIVER, AT LEAST?
YES! THEY'RE WEST OF THE NURU!
THAT'S RIGHT.

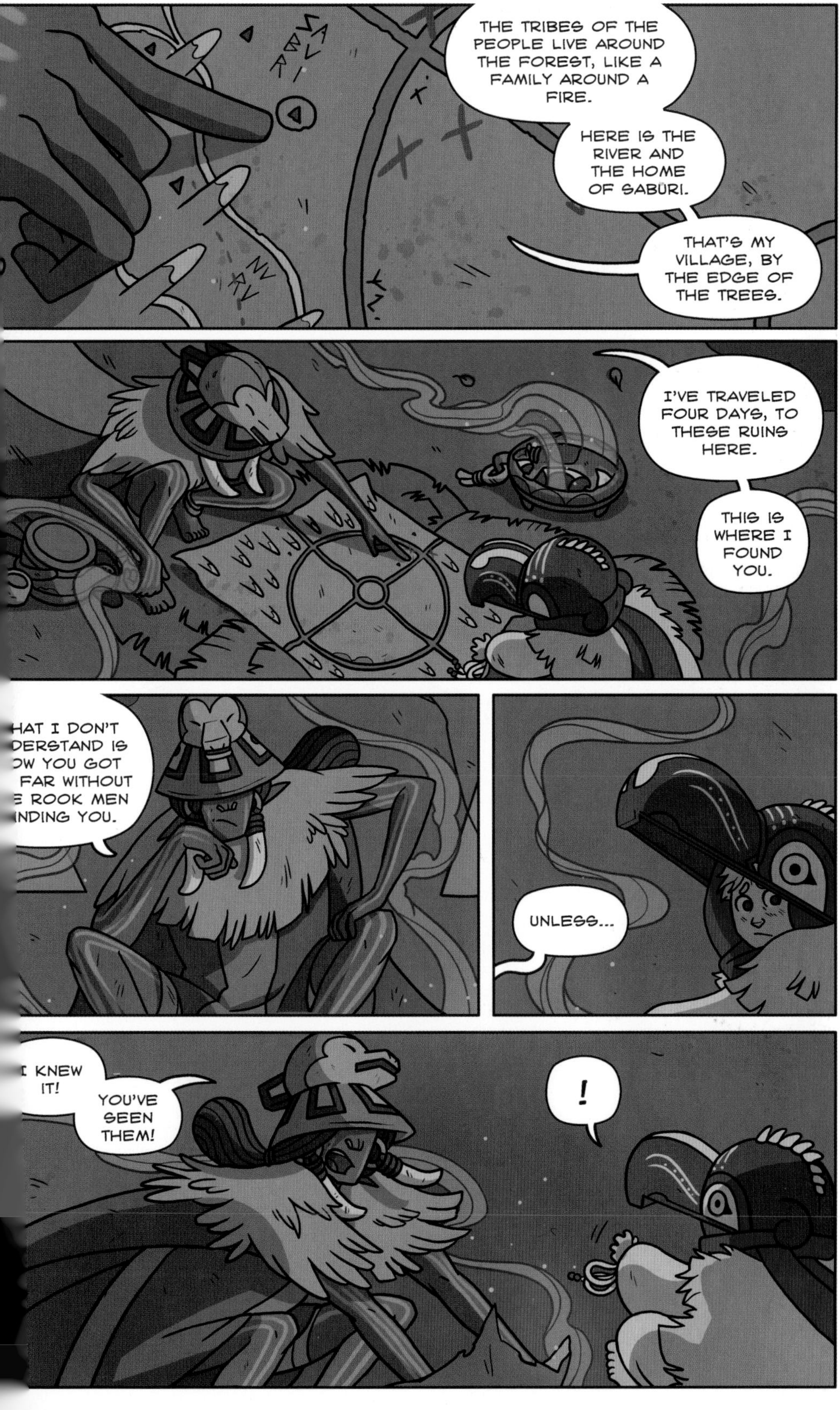
THE TRIBES OF THE PEOPLE LIVE AROUND THE FOREST, LIKE A FAMILY AROUND A FIRE.
HERE IS THE RIVER AND THE HOME OF SABŪRI.
THAT'S MY VILLAGE, BY THE EDGE OF THE TREES.
I'VE TRAVELED FOUR DAYS, TO THESE RUINS HERE.
THIS IS WHERE I FOUND YOU.
HAT I DON'T DERSTAND IS OW YOU GOT FAR WITHOUT E ROOK MEN NDING YOU.
UNLESS...
I KNEW IT!
YOU'VE SEEN THEM!
!

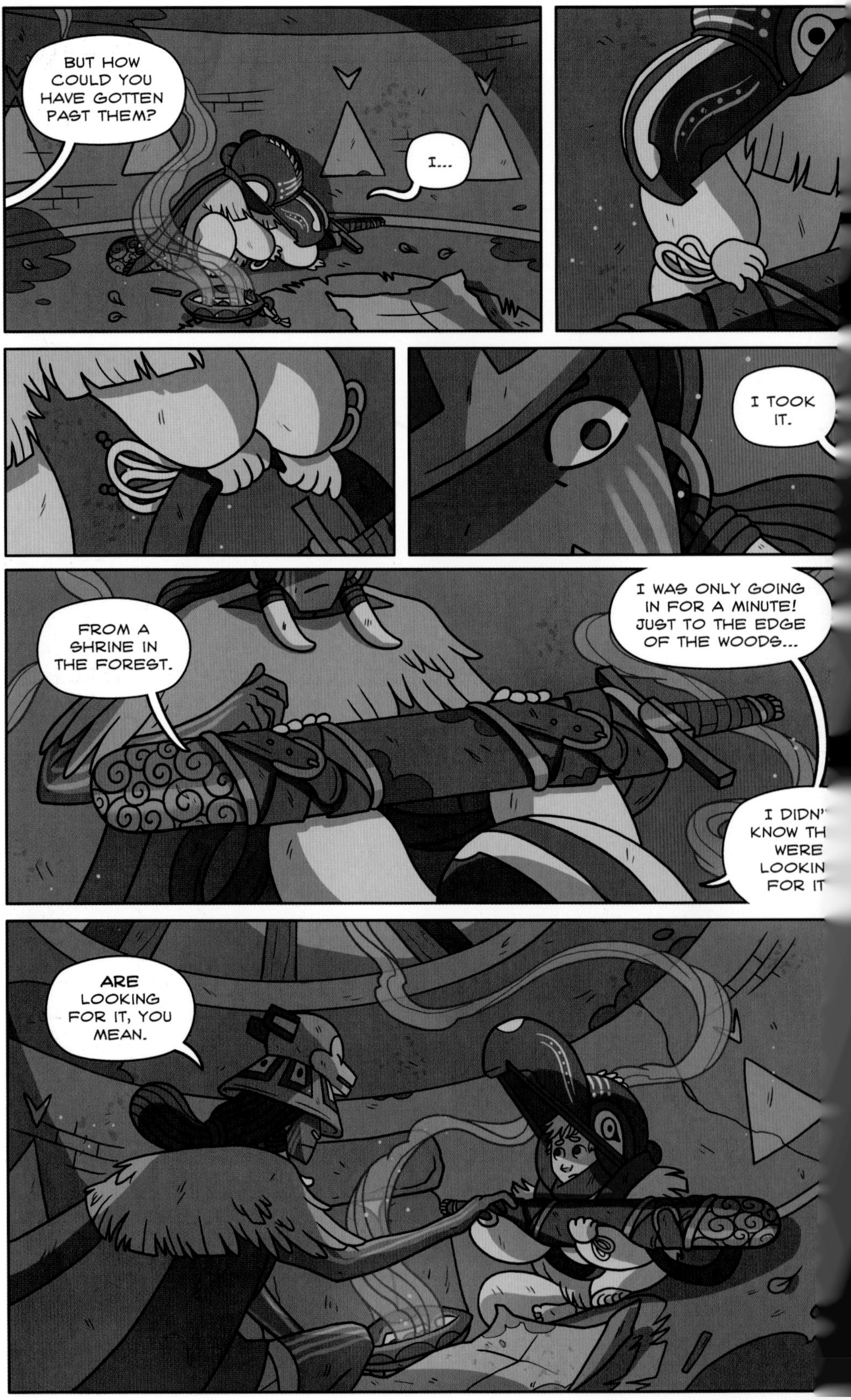
BUT HOW COULD YOU HAVE GOTTEN PAST THEM?
I...
I TOOK IT.
FROM A SHRINE IN THE FOREST.
I WAS ONLY GOING IN FOR A MINUTE! JUST TO THE EDGE OF THE WOODS...
I DIDN' KNOW TH WERE LOOKIN FOR IT
ARE LOOKING FOR IT, YOU MEAN.

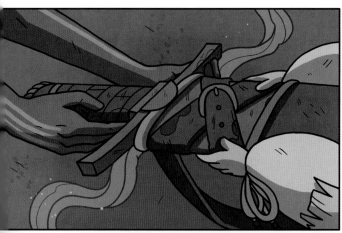

SO THIS IS WHY THEY'VE BEEN COMING SO CLOSE TO THE EDGE OF THE WOODS...

"HE LURED THE HALF-WAY BEAST DEEP INTO THE LIMINAL WOOD...

"AND CUT HIM DOWN WITH BELL AND SWORD..."

RATTLE

WHA--?!

IT'S STUCK PRETTY GOOD. LOOKS LIKE THE SCABBARD'S BEEN WARPED.

BUT IT OPENED EARLIER!

THERE WAS A BIG LIGHT!

AND THEN I FELL INTO THE WATER...

THAT'S HOW I GOT LOST...

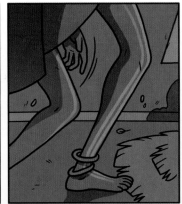

WELL...

...NIGHTTIME IS NO TIME FOR TRAVELING AROUND HERE...

SO WHY DON'T YOU REST WHILE YOU CAN.

SHIFF

WE'LL TALK ABOUT WHAT WE CAN DO IN THE MORNING.

OKAY?

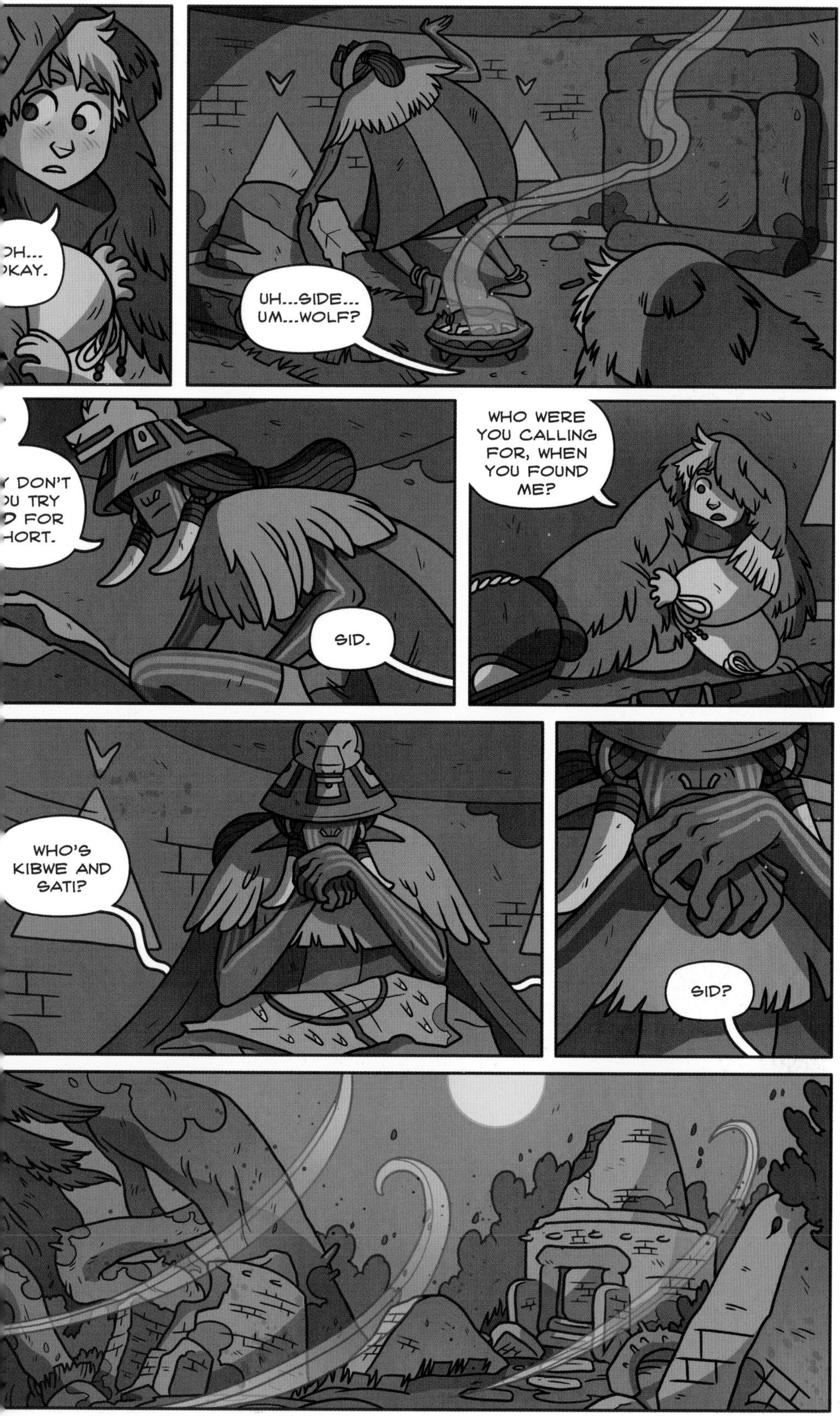

H... KAY.
UH...SIDE... UM...WOLF?
DON'T U TRY D FOR HORT.
SID.
WHO WERE YOU CALLING FOR, WHEN YOU FOUND ME?
WHO'S KIBWE AND SATI?
SID?

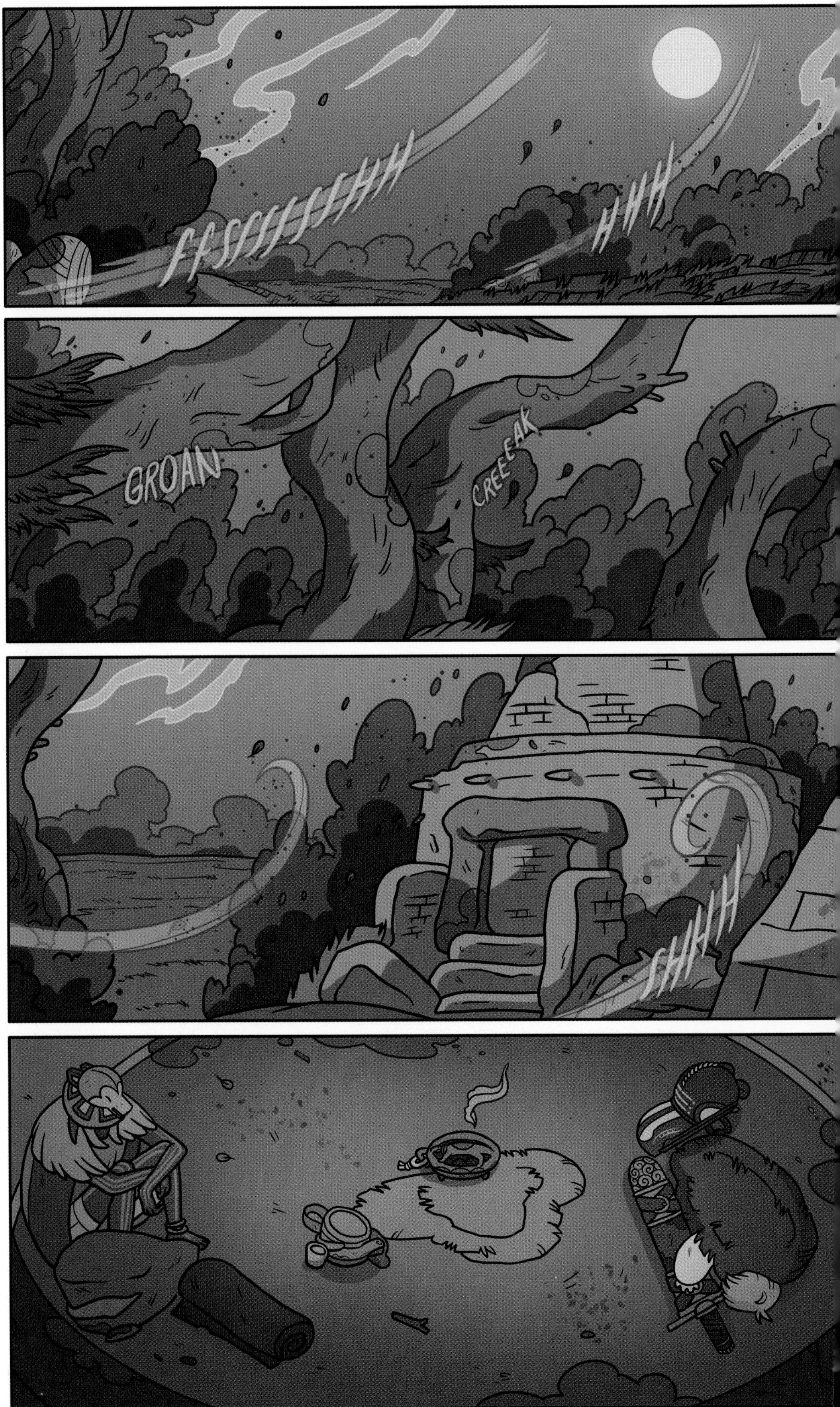
FFSSSSSSSHHH
HHH
GROAN
CREEEAK
SHHH

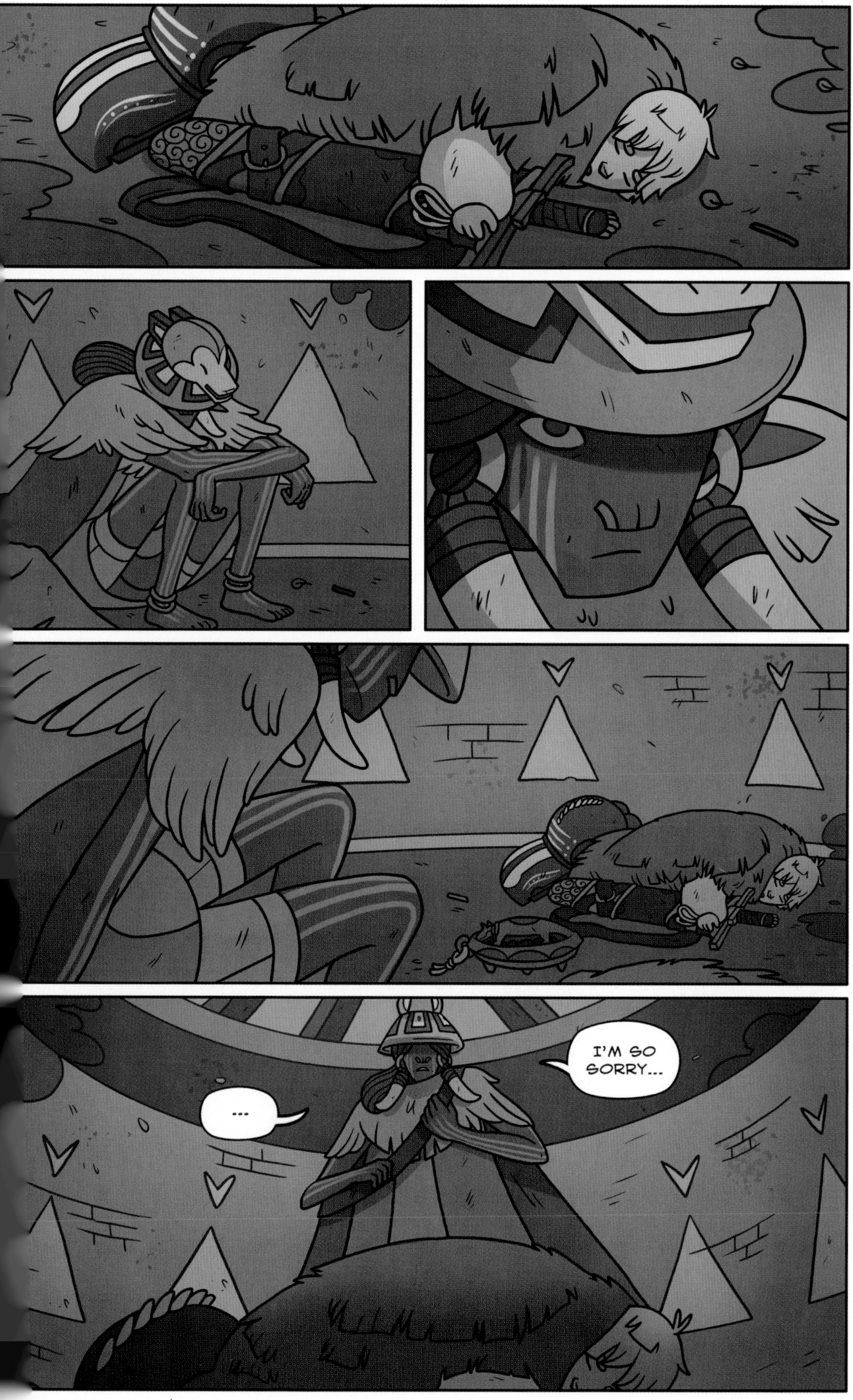
...
I'M SO SORRY...

I'LL COME BACK FOR YOU IF I CAN.

BUT THERE'S SOMETHING I HAVE TO DO FIRST...

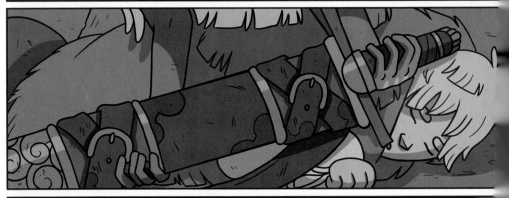

I'VE COME TOO FAR TO TURN BACK NOW...

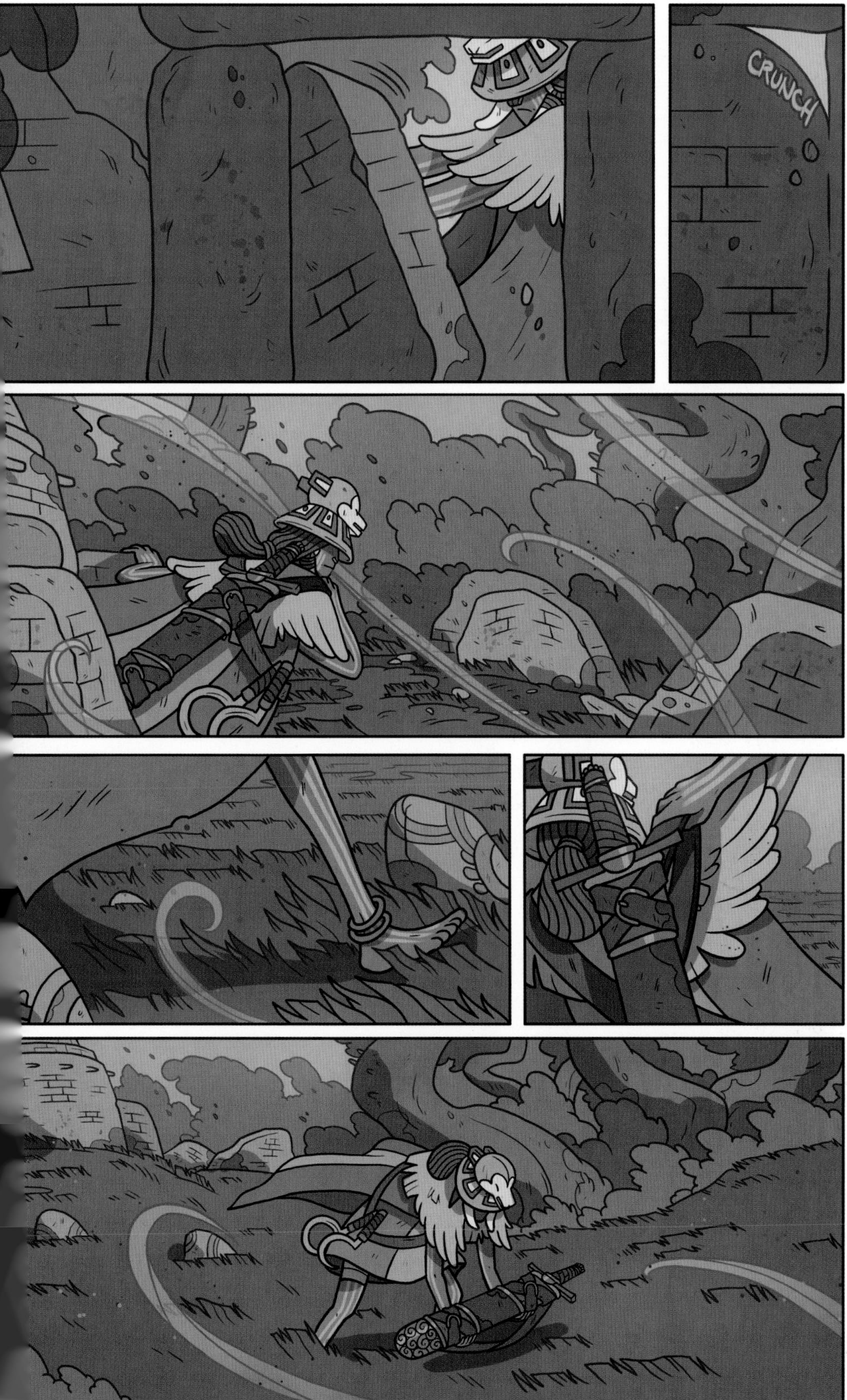
CRUNCH

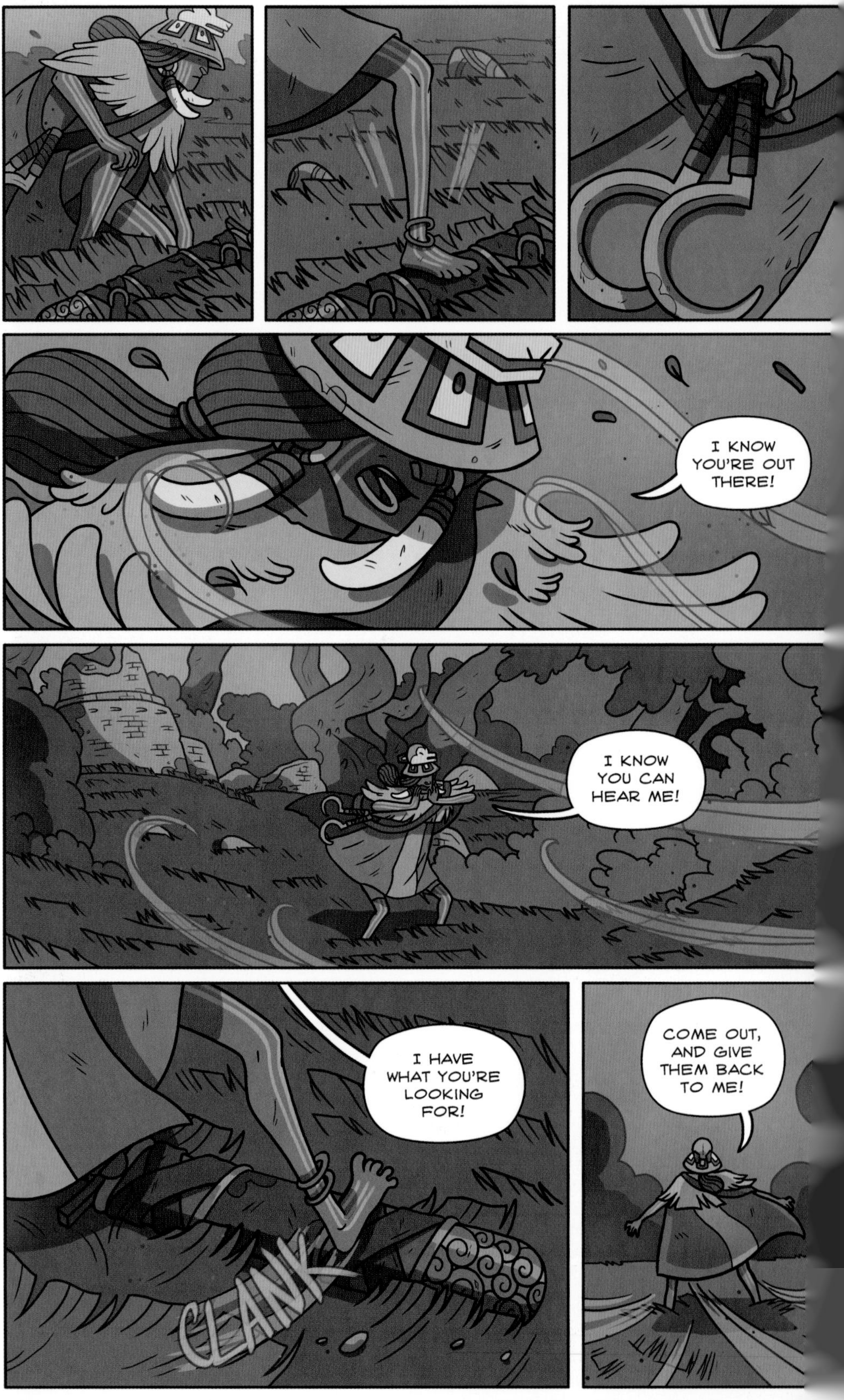
I KNOW YOU'RE OUT THERE!
I KNOW YOU CAN HEAR ME!
I HAVE WHAT YOU'RE LOOKING FOR!
CLANK
COME OUT, AND GIVE THEM BACK TO ME!

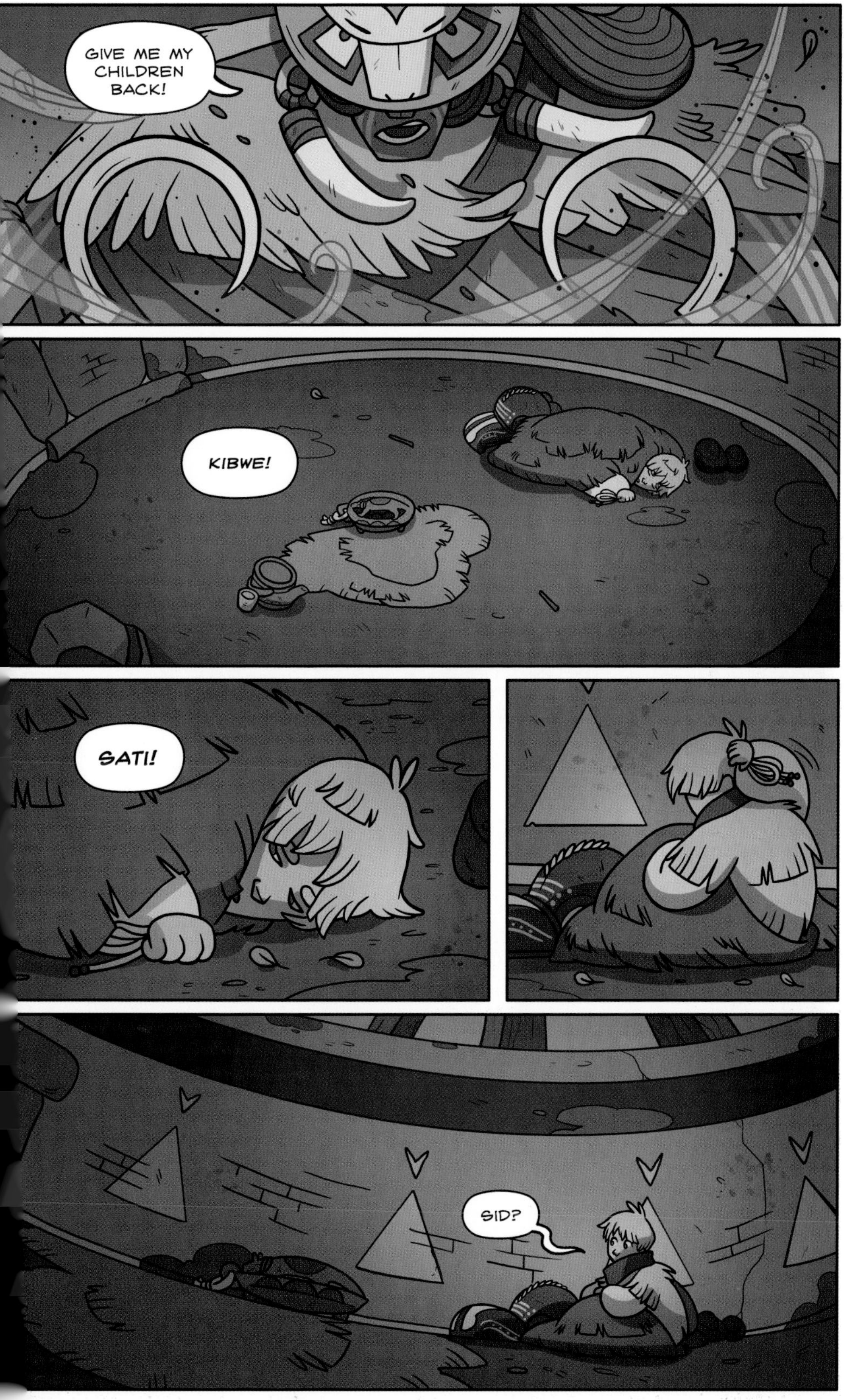
GIVE ME MY CHILDREN BACK!
KIBWE!
SATI!
SID?

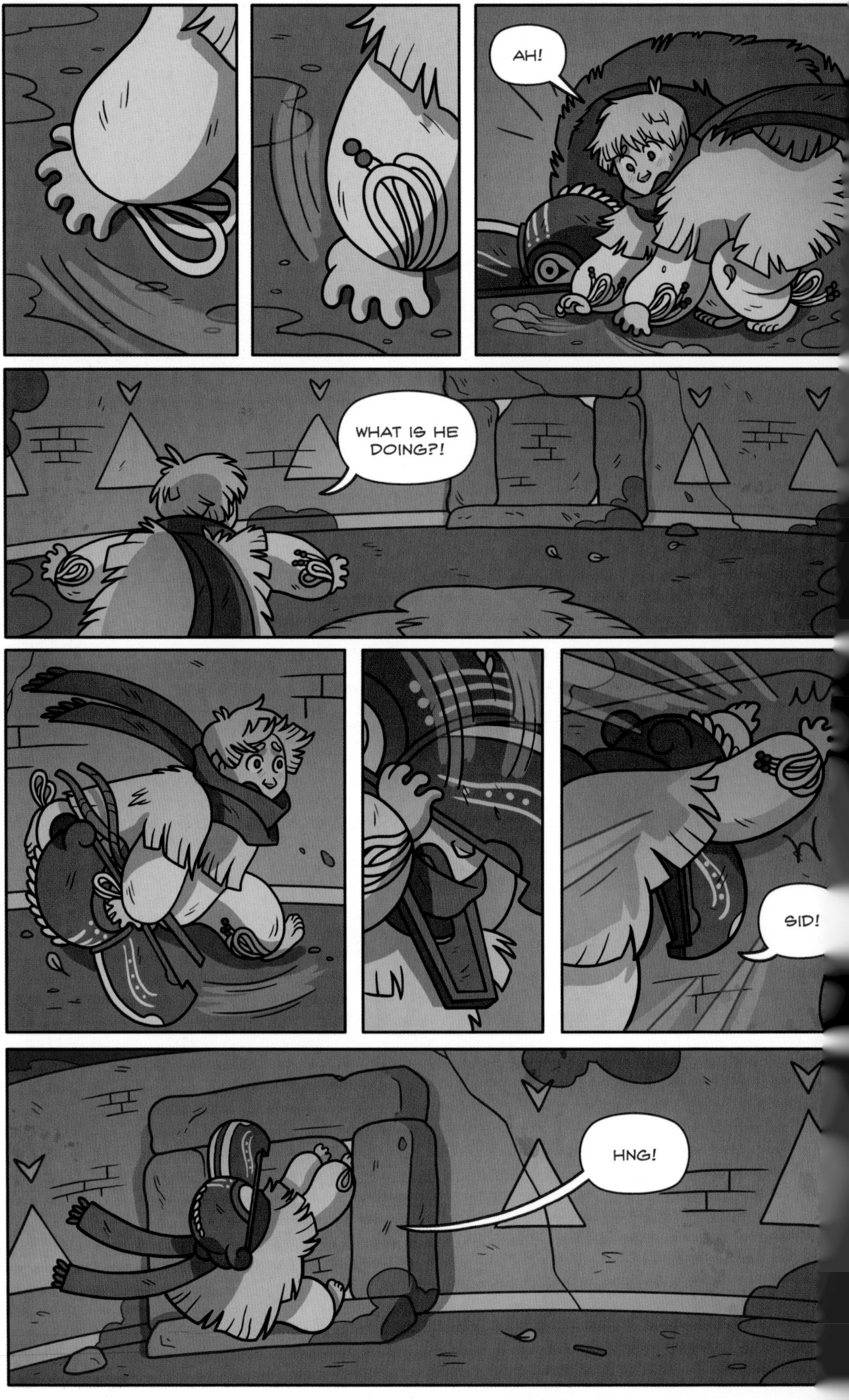
AH!
WHAT IS HE DOING?!
SID!
HNG!

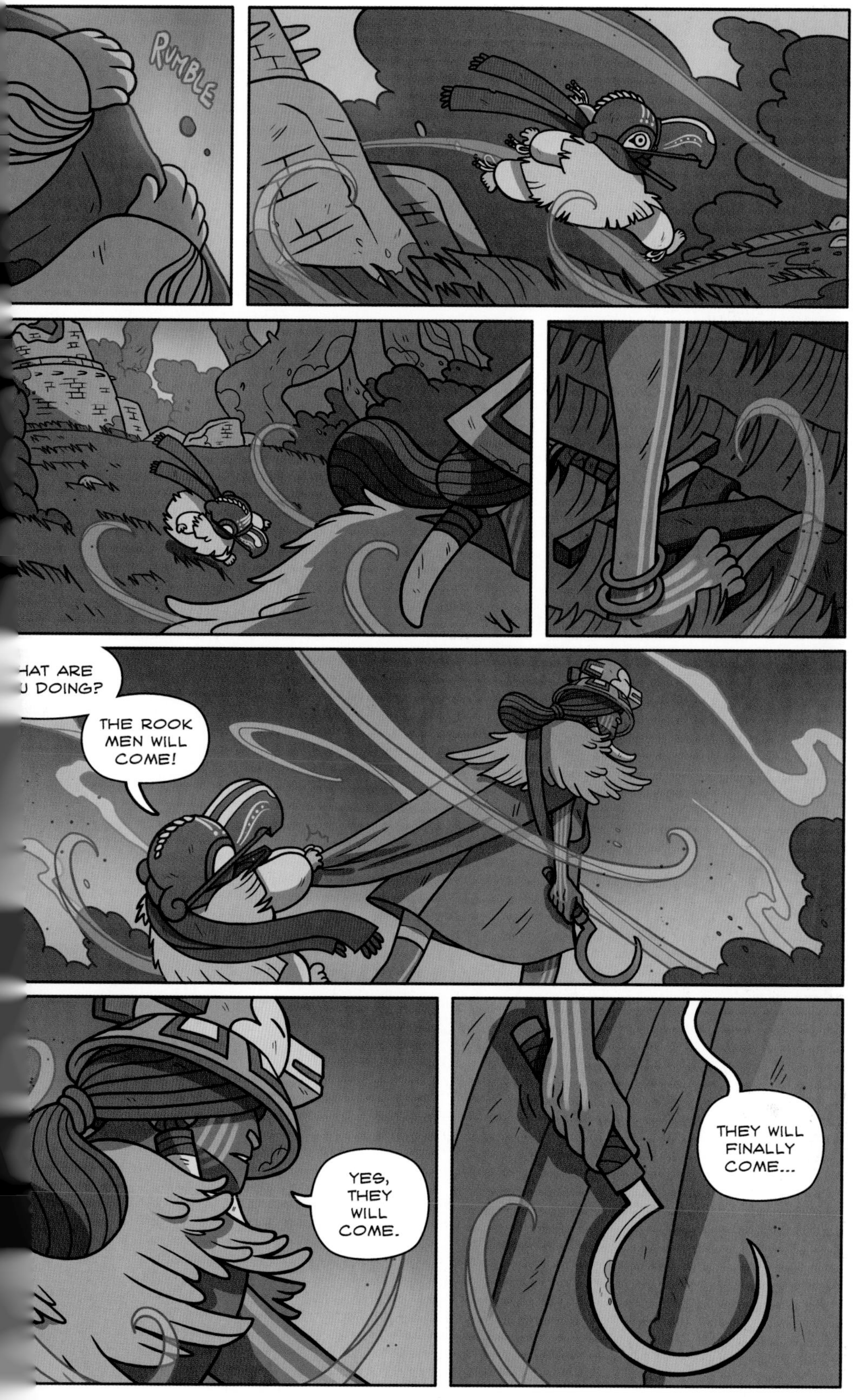
RUMBLE
HAT ARE
U DOING?
THE ROOK
MEN WILL
COME!
YES,
THEY
WILL
COME.
THEY WILL
FINALLY
COME...

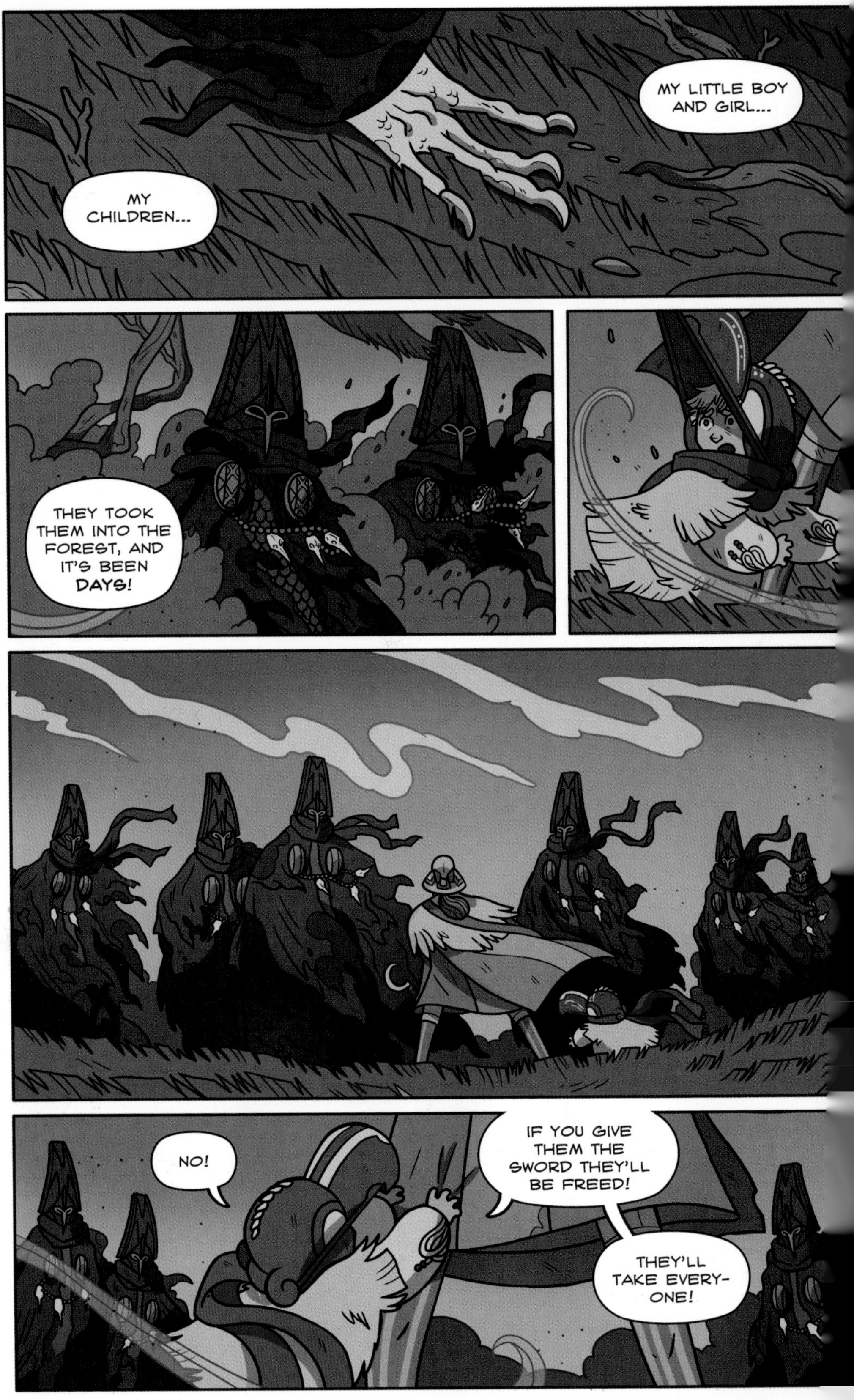
MY CHILDREN...
MY LITTLE BOY AND GIRL...
THEY TOOK THEM INTO THE FOREST, AND IT'S BEEN **DAYS!**
NO!
IF YOU GIVE THEM THE SWORD THEY'LL BE FREED!
THEY'LL TAKE EVERY-ONE!

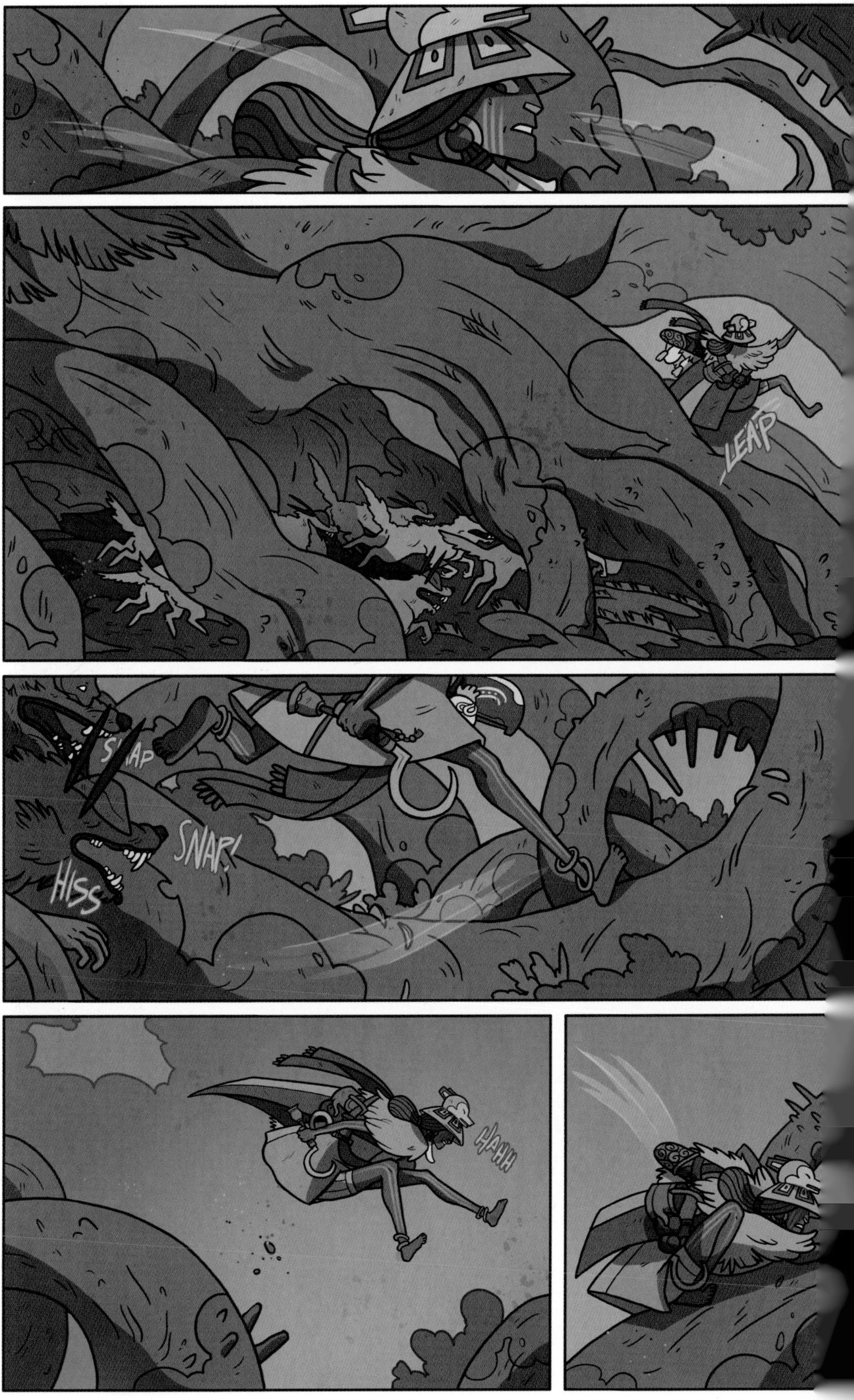
LEAP
SNAP
SNAP!
HISS
HAHH

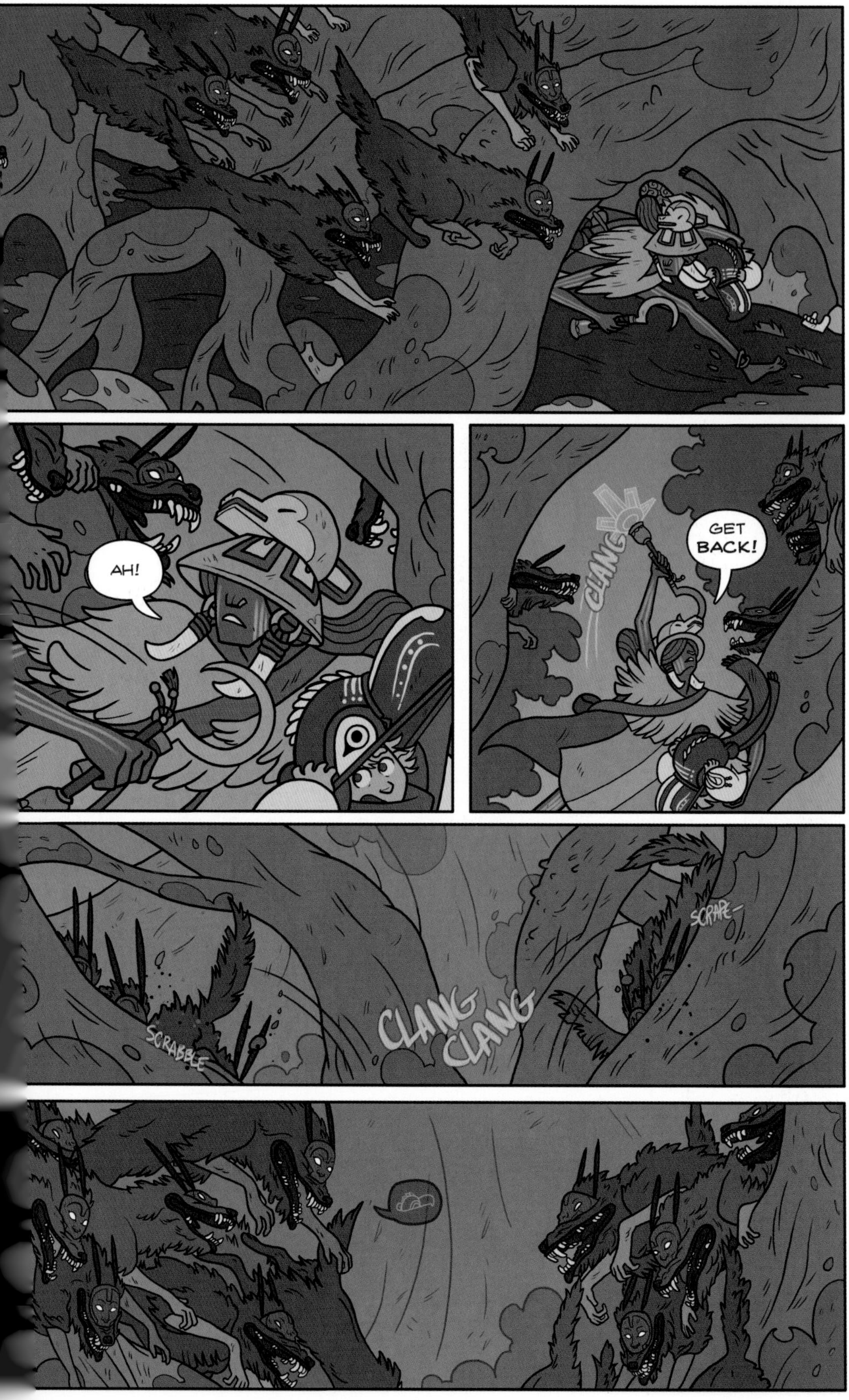
AH!
CLANG
GET BACK!
SCRABBLE
CLANG CLANG
SCRAPE-

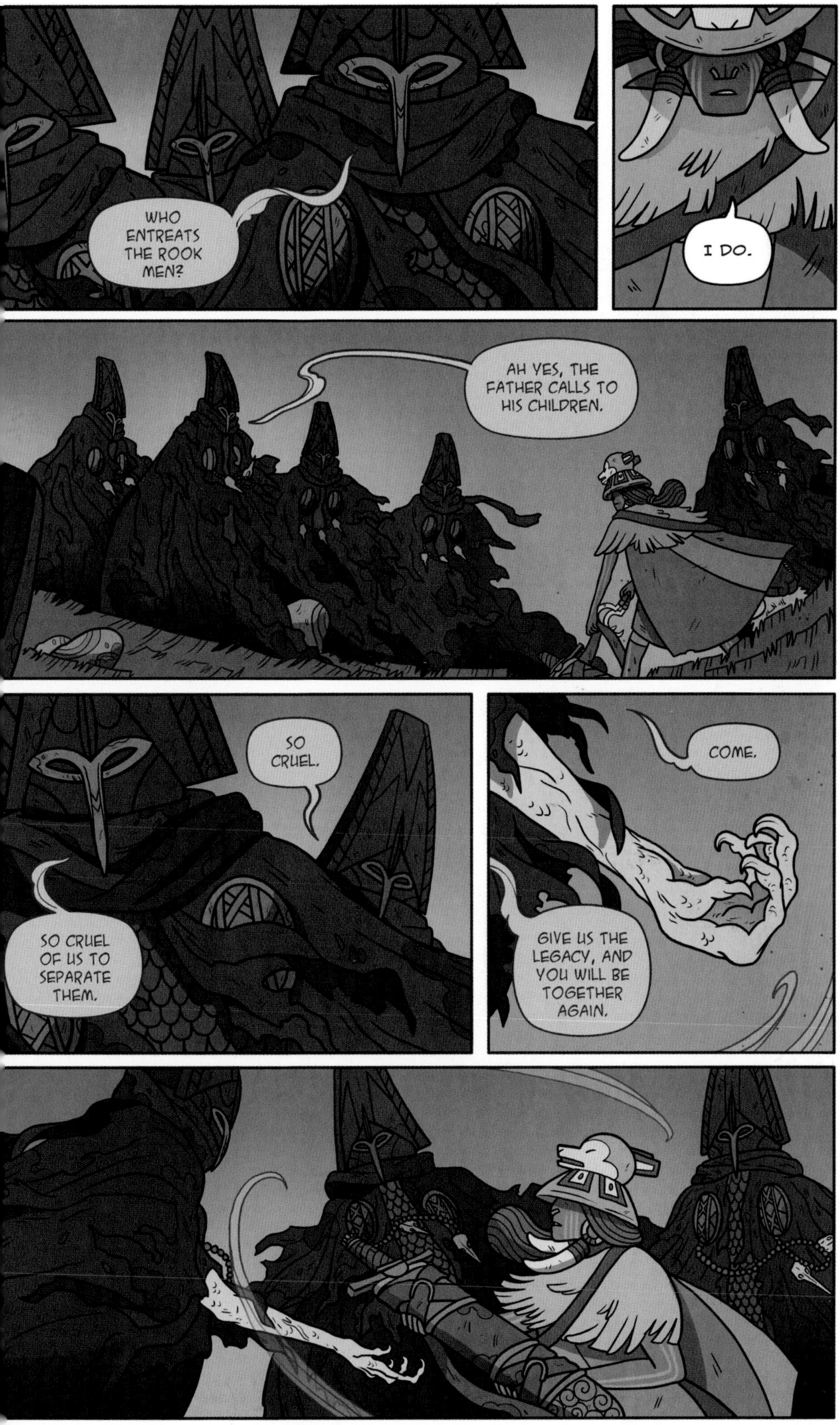
WHO ENTREATS THE ROOK MEN?
I DO.
AH YES, THE FATHER CALLS TO HIS CHILDREN.
SO CRUEL.
SO CRUEL OF US TO SEPARATE THEM.
COME.
GIVE US THE LEGACY, AND YOU WILL BE TOGETHER AGAIN.

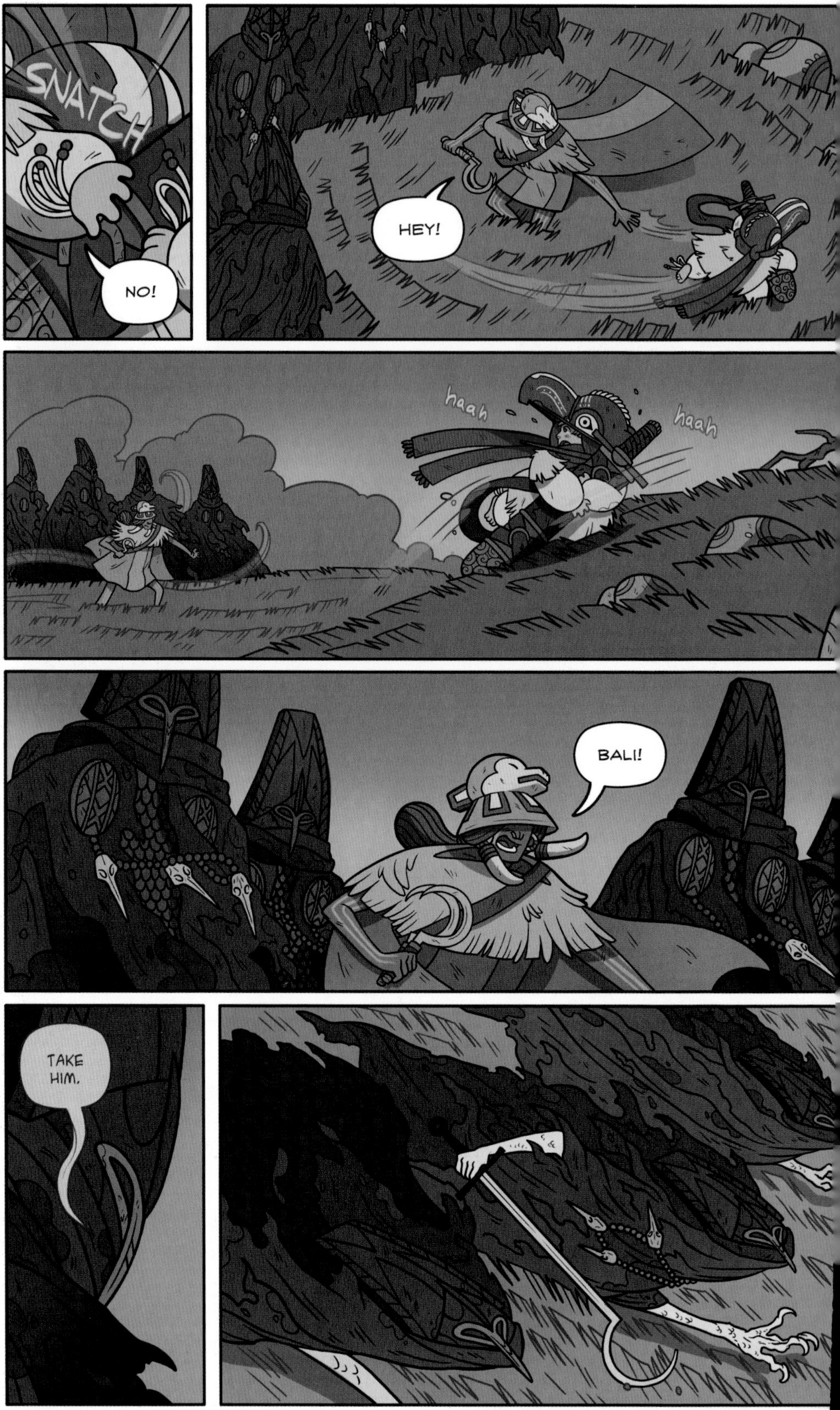
SNATCH
NO!
HEY!
haah
haah
BALI!
TAKE HIM.

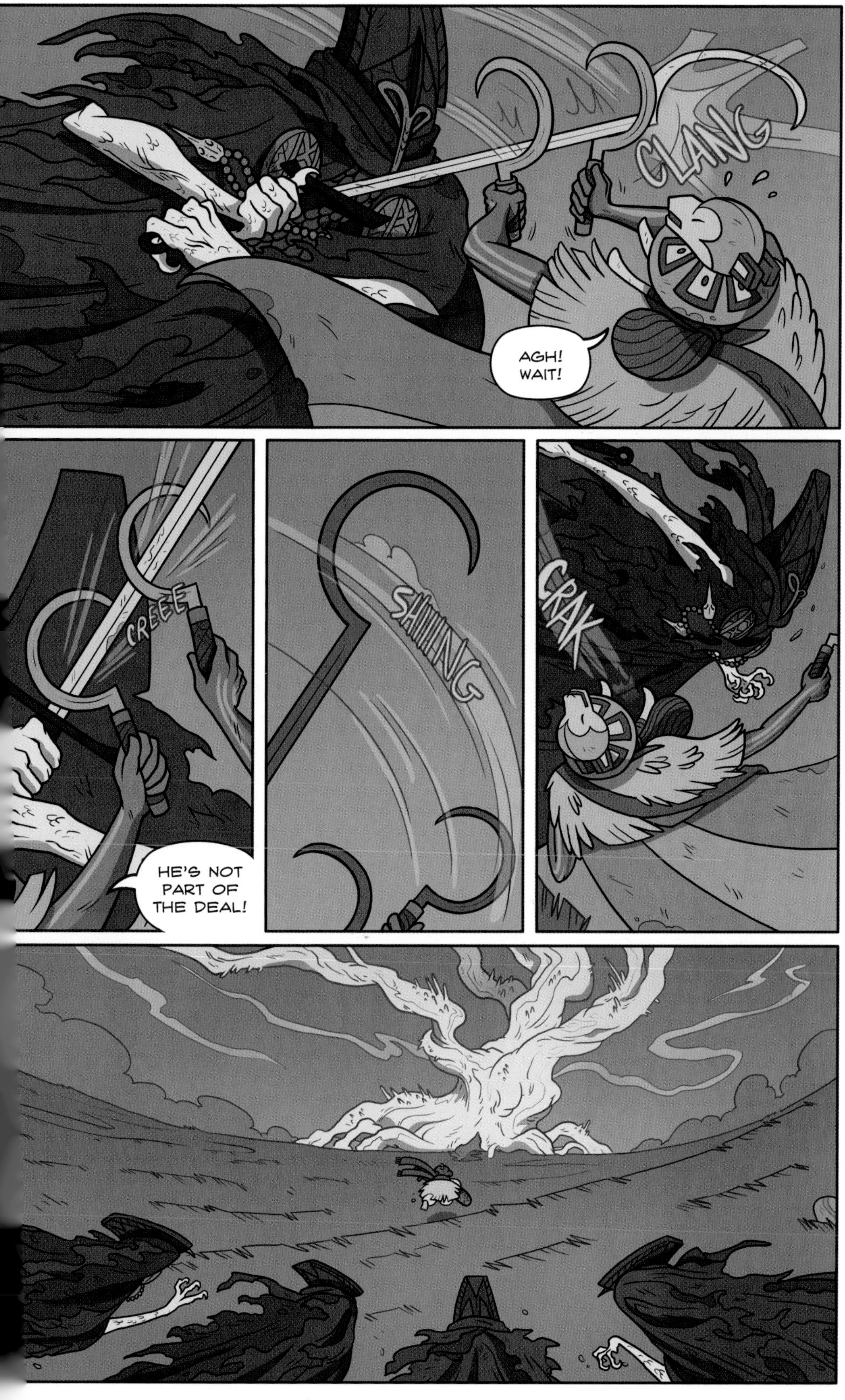
CLANG
AGH! WAIT!
CREEE
HE'S NOT PART OF THE DEAL!
SHIIING
CRAK

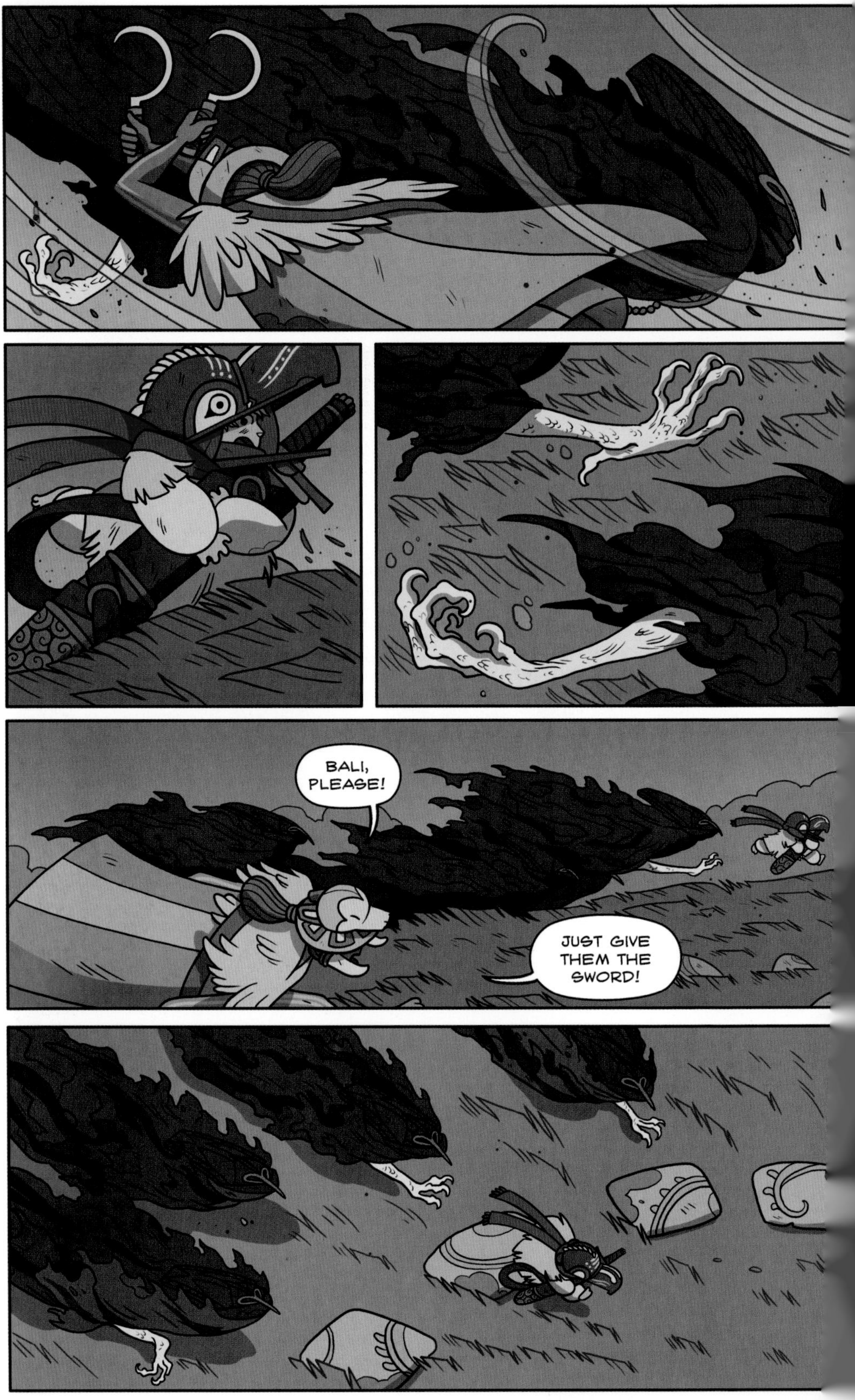
BALI,
PLEASE!
JUST GIVE
THEM THE
SWORD!

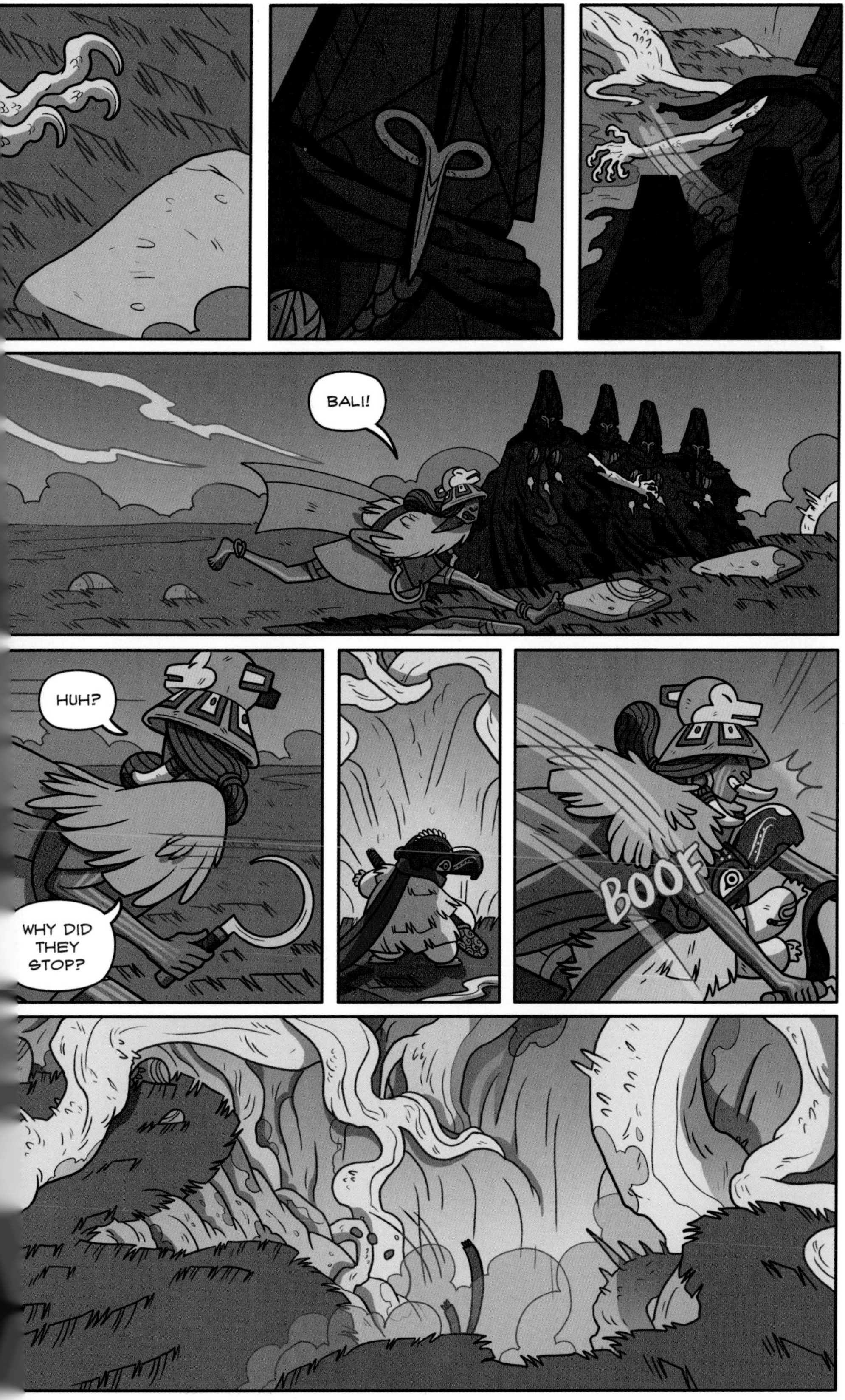
BALI!
HUH?
WHY DID THEY STOP?
BOOF

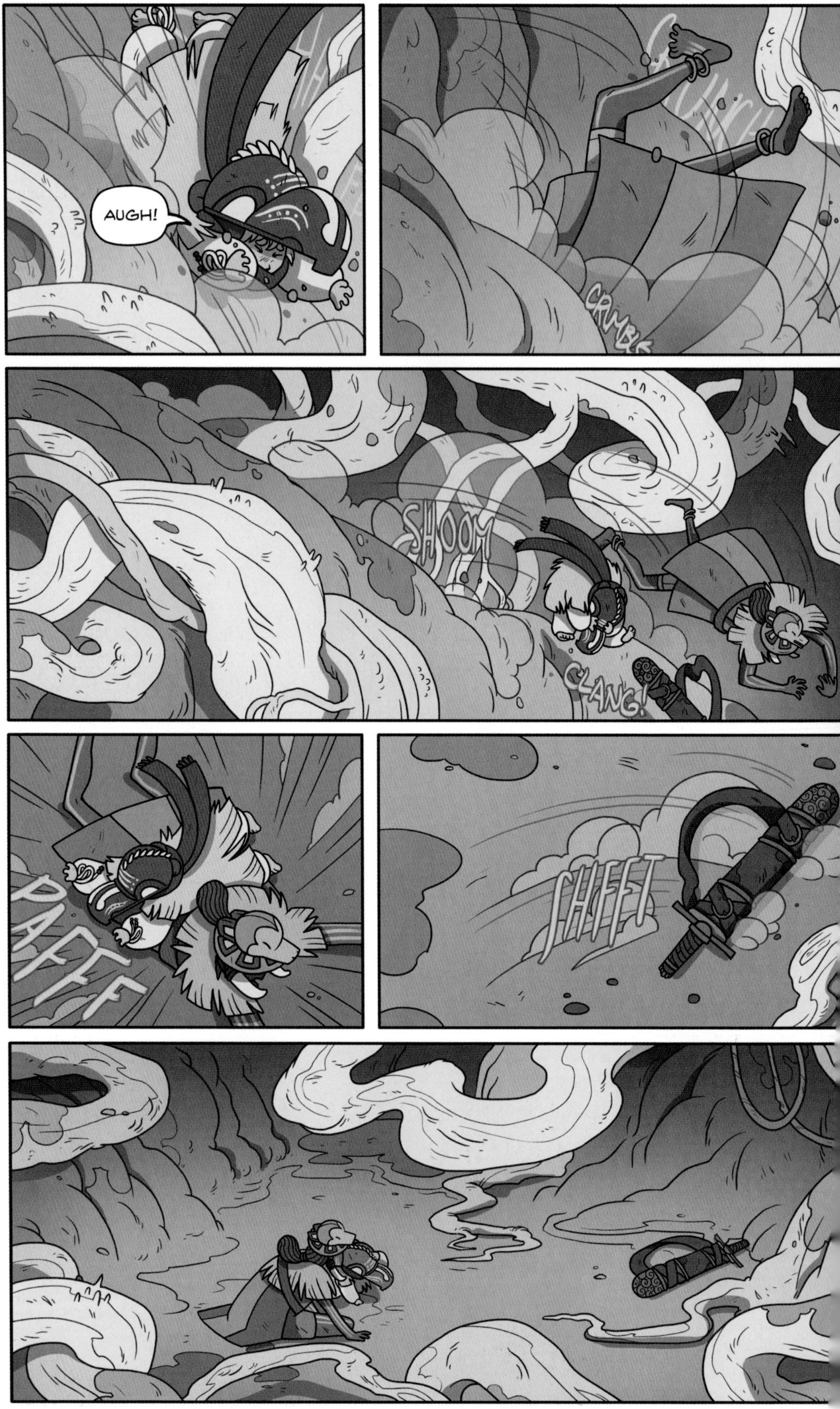
AUGH!
SHOOM
CLANG!
PAFFF
SHFFT

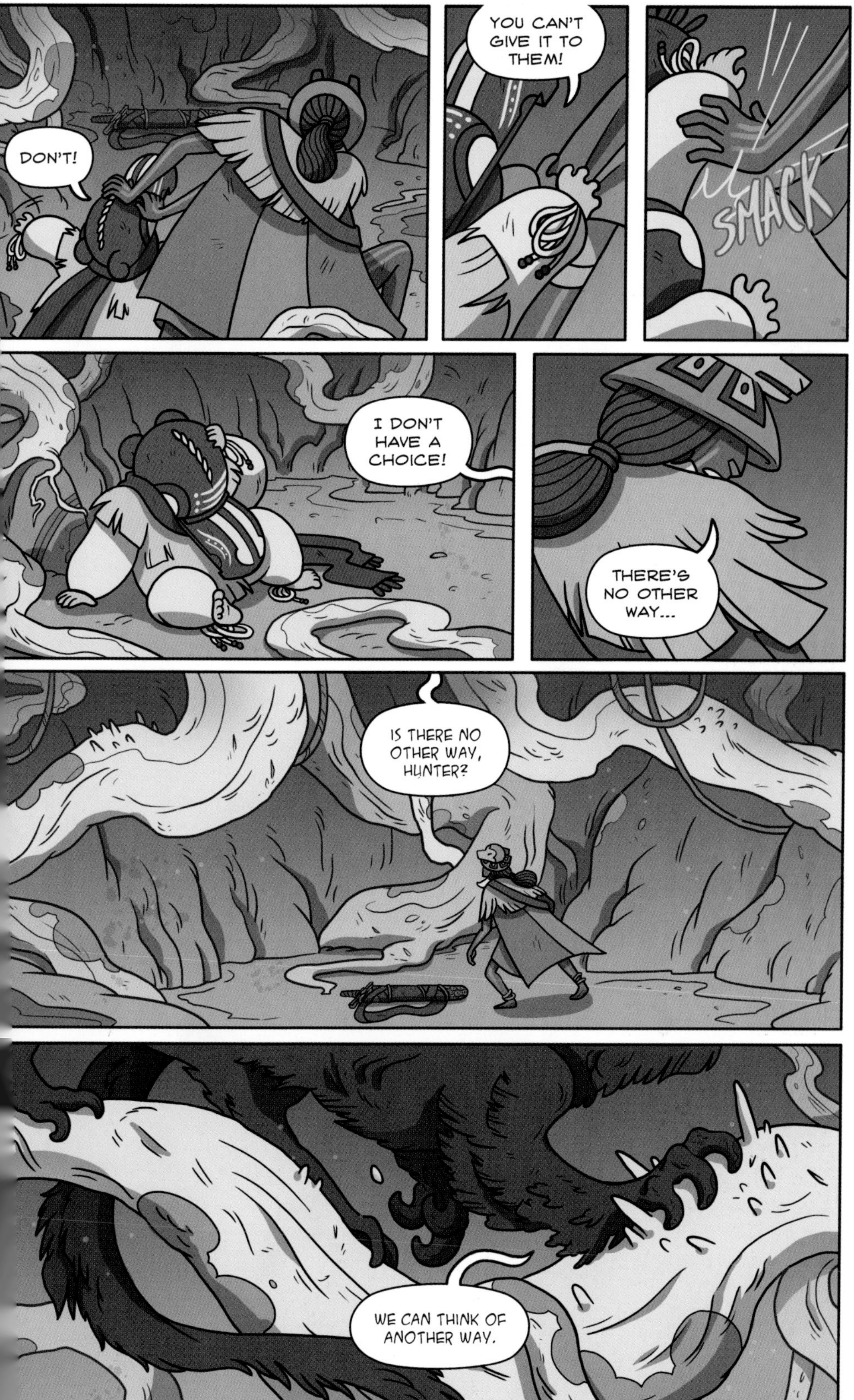
DON'T!
YOU CAN'T GIVE IT TO THEM!
SMACK
I DON'T HAVE A CHOICE!
THERE'S NO OTHER WAY...
IS THERE NO OTHER WAY, HUNTER?
WE CAN THINK OF ANOTHER WAY.

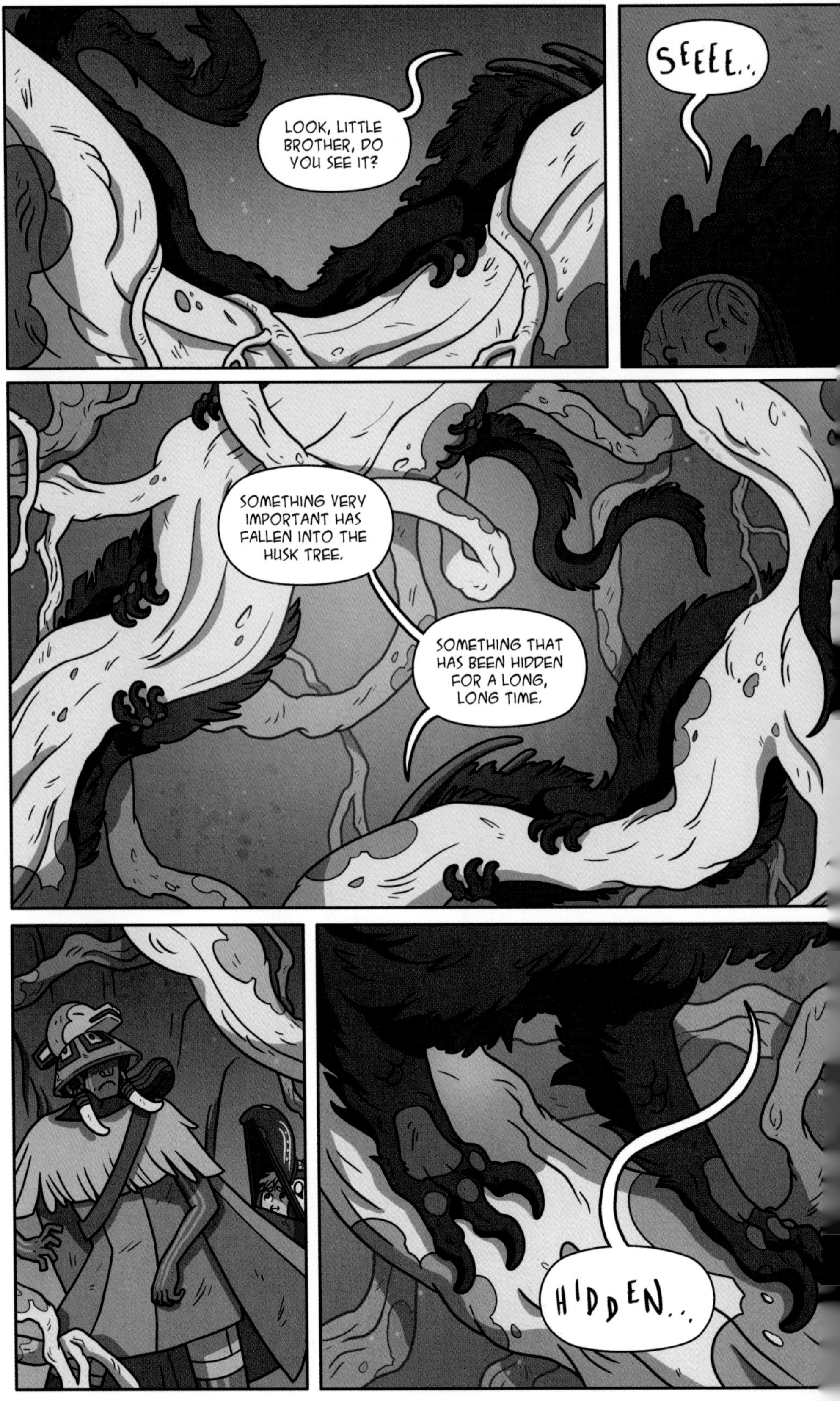
LOOK, LITTLE BROTHER, DO YOU SEE IT?
SEEEE...
SOMETHING VERY IMPORTANT HAS FALLEN INTO THE HUSK TREE.
SOMETHING THAT HAS BEEN HIDDEN FOR A LONG, LONG TIME.
HIDDEN...

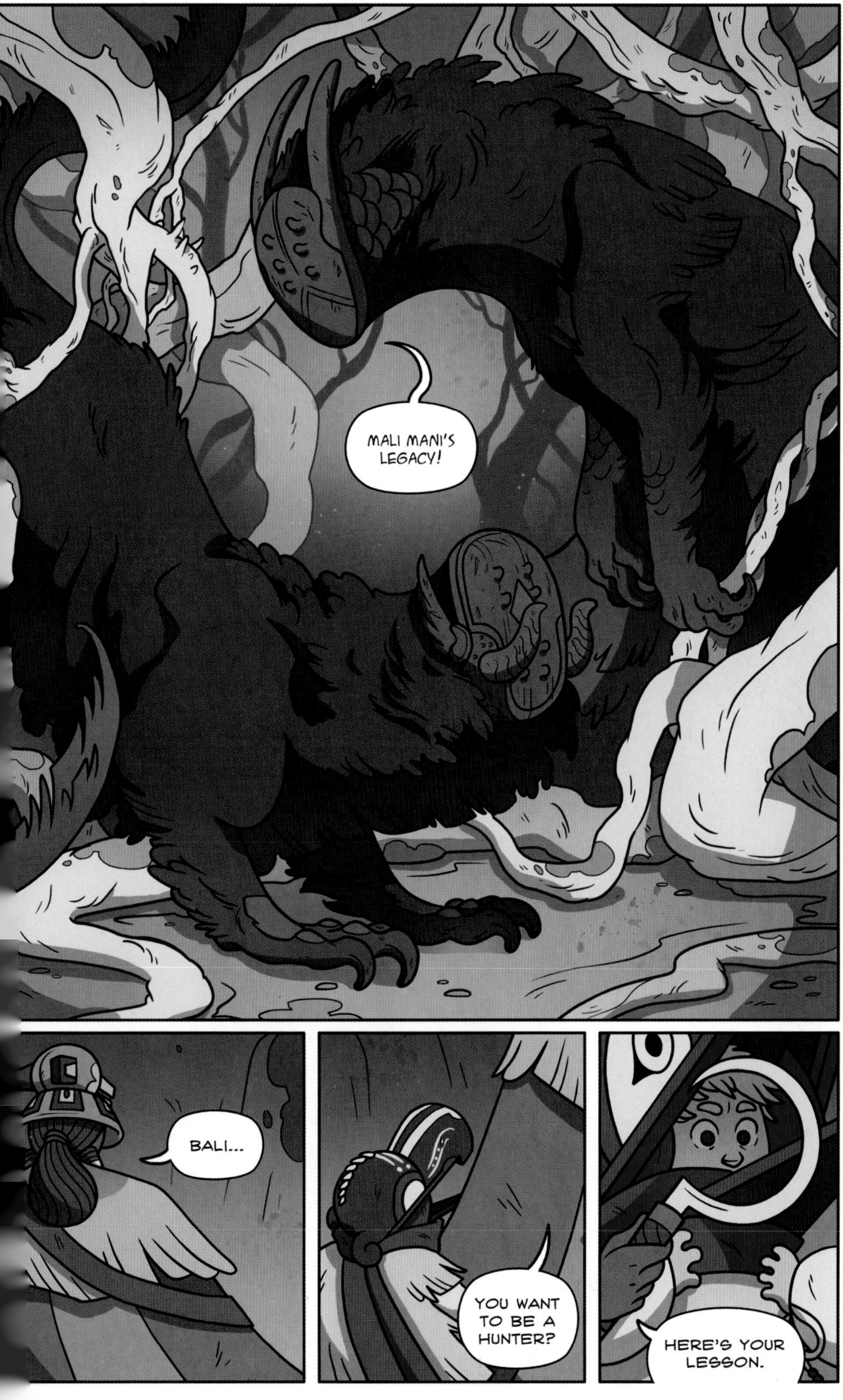
MALI MANI'S LEGACY!
BALI...
YOU WANT TO BE A HUNTER?
HERE'S YOUR LESSON.

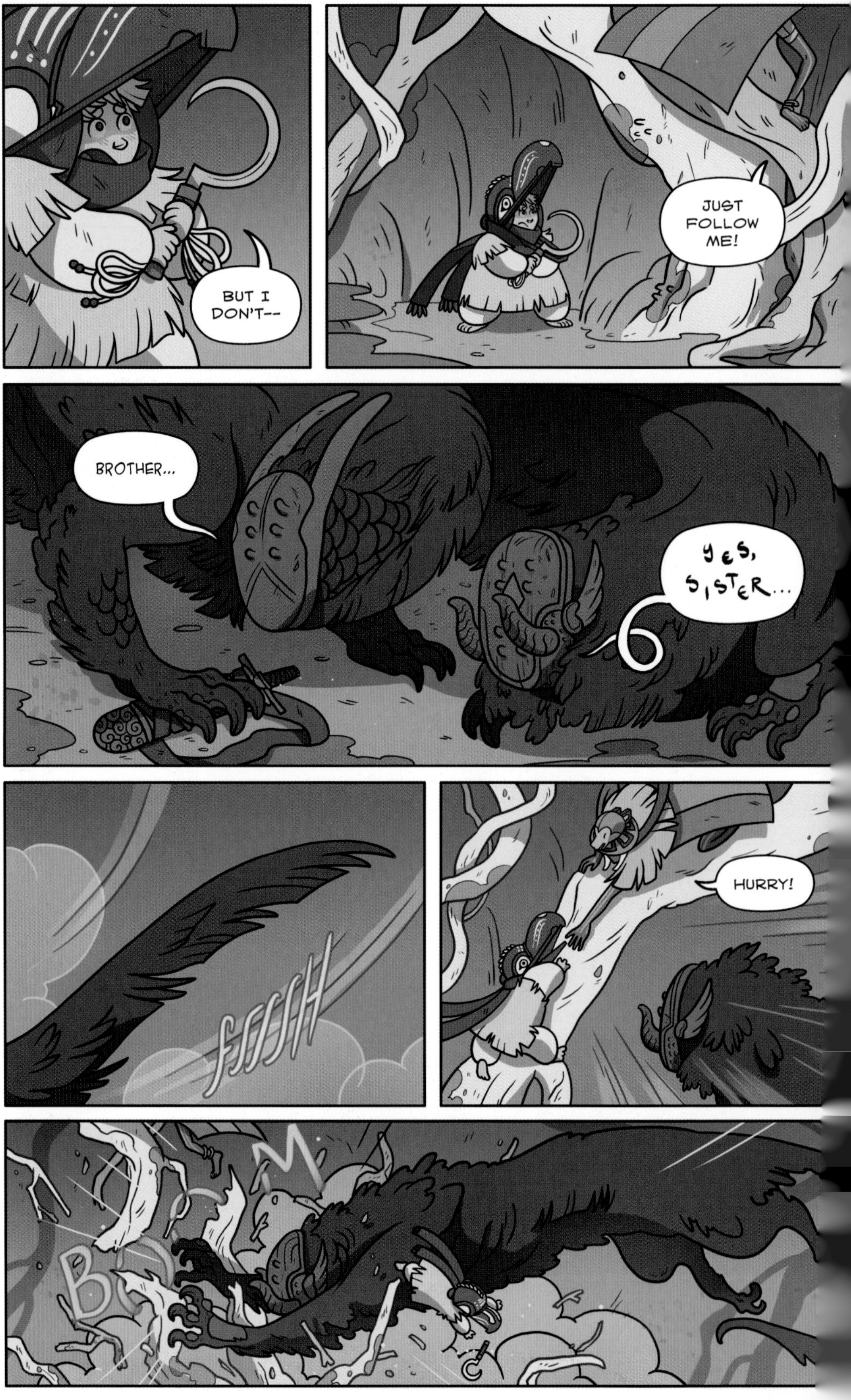
BUT I DON'T--
JUST FOLLOW ME!
BROTHER...
YES, SISTER...
HURRY!

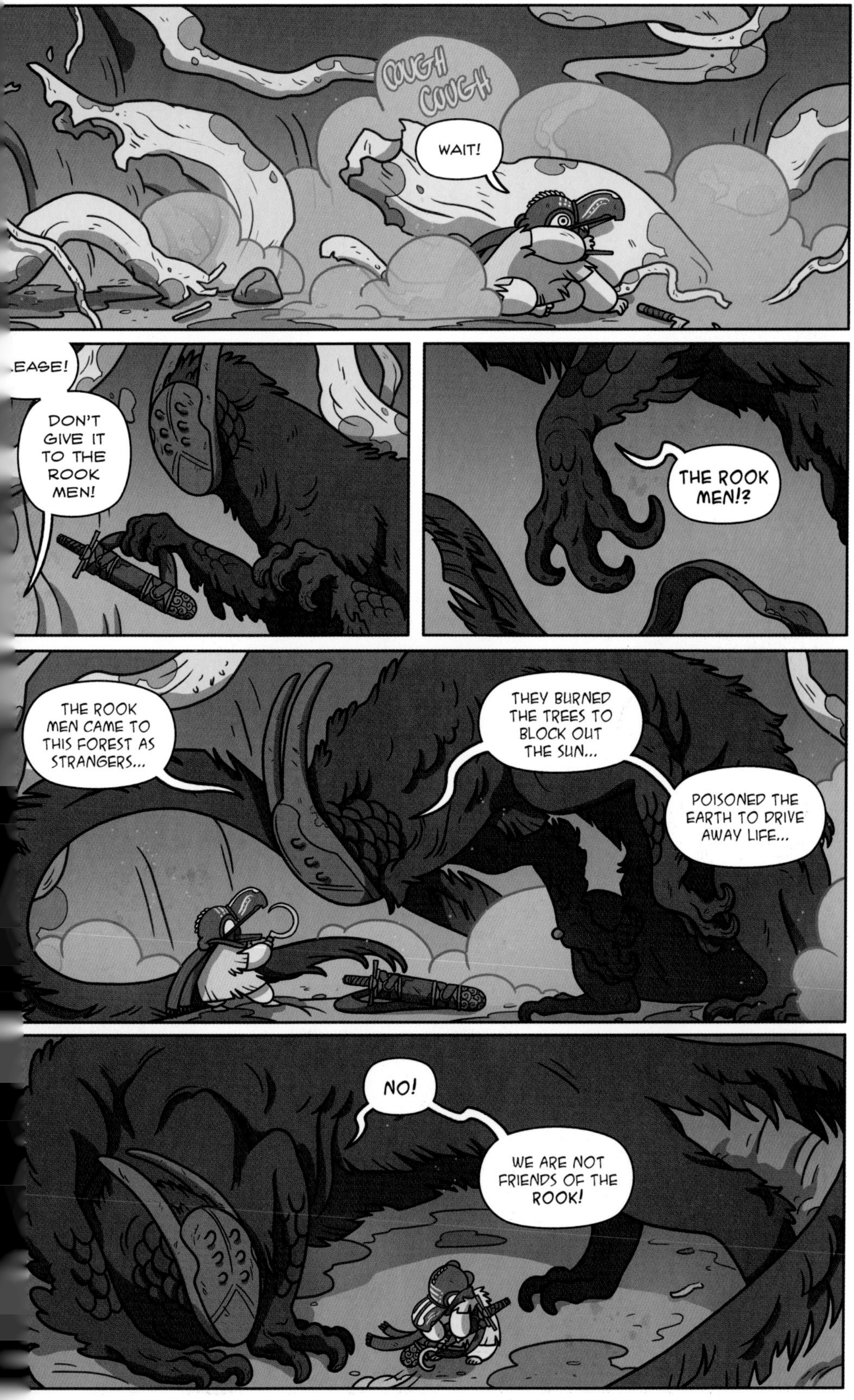

COUGH COUGH
WAIT!
EASE!
DON'T GIVE IT TO THE ROOK MEN!
THE ROOK MEN!?
THE ROOK MEN CAME TO THIS FOREST AS STRANGERS...
THEY BURNED THE TREES TO BLOCK OUT THE SUN...
POISONED THE EARTH TO DRIVE AWAY LIFE...
NO!
WE ARE NOT FRIENDS OF THE ROOK!

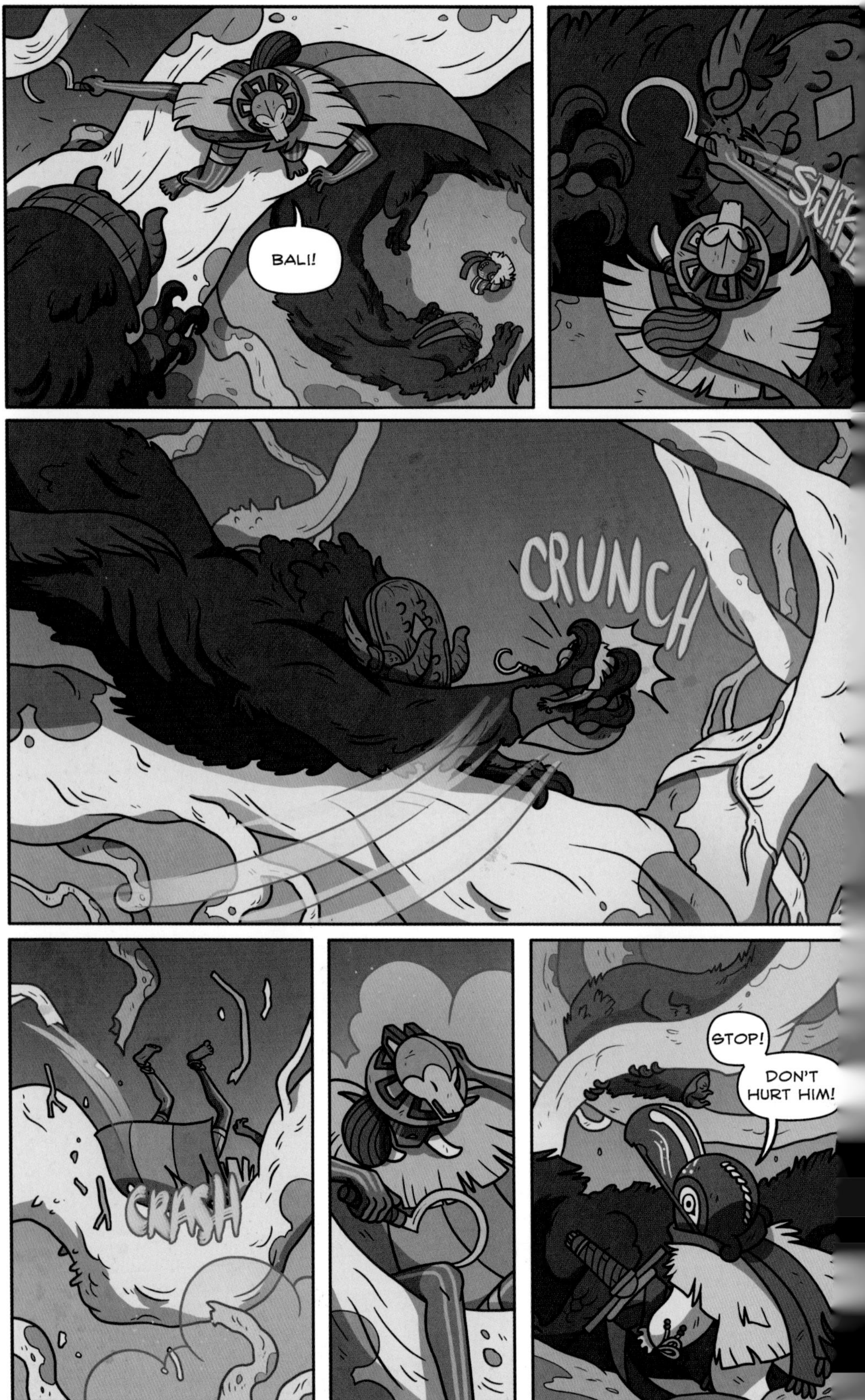
BALI!
SWIF
CRUNCH
CRASH
STOP!
DON'T HURT HIM!

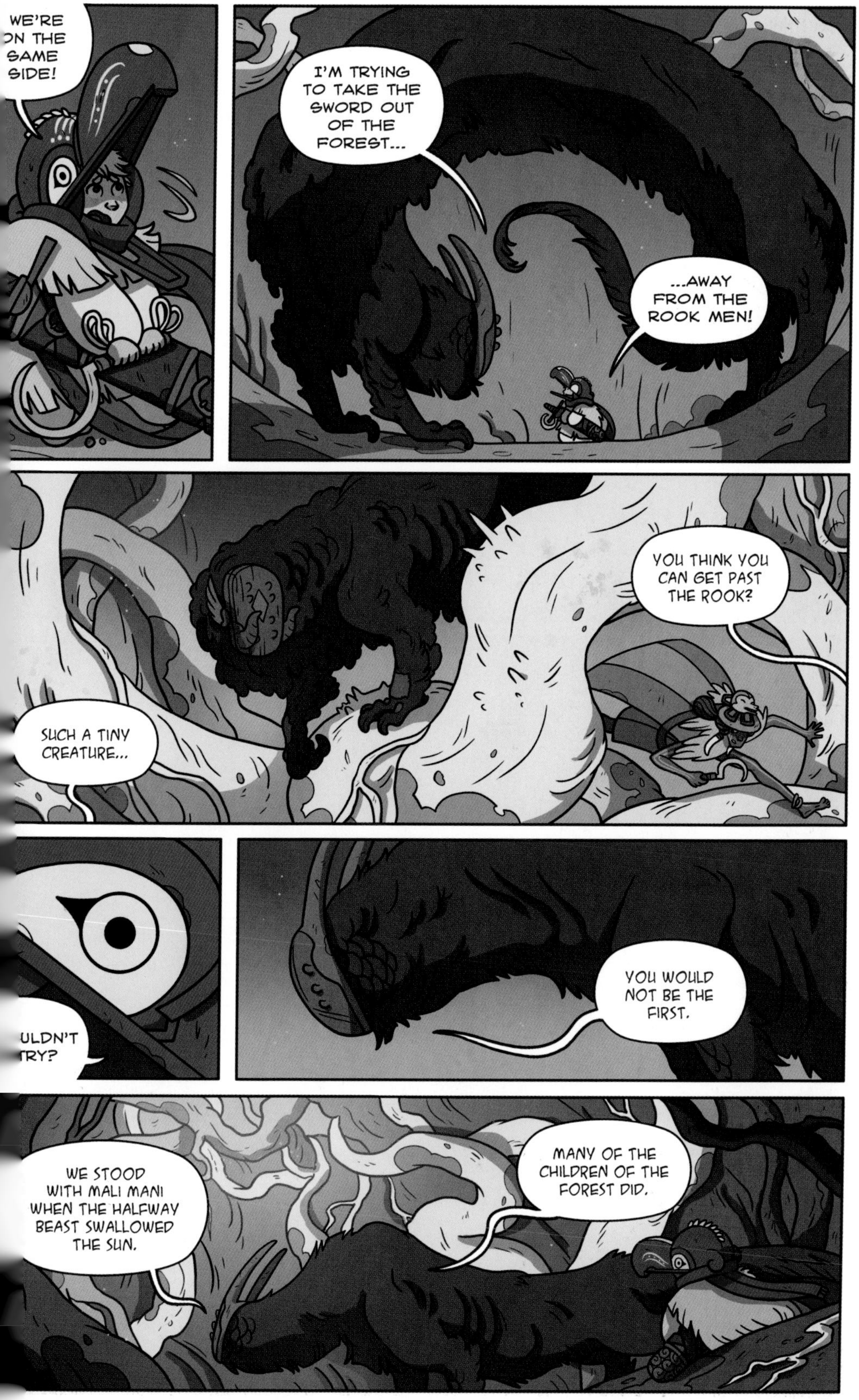
WE'RE ON THE SAME SIDE!
I'M TRYING TO TAKE THE SWORD OUT OF THE FOREST...
...AWAY FROM THE ROOK MEN!
YOU THINK YOU CAN GET PAST THE ROOK?
SUCH A TINY CREATURE...
ULDN'T TRY?
YOU WOULD NOT BE THE FIRST.
WE STOOD WITH MALI MANI WHEN THE HALFWAY BEAST SWALLOWED THE SUN.
MANY OF THE CHILDREN OF THE FOREST DID.

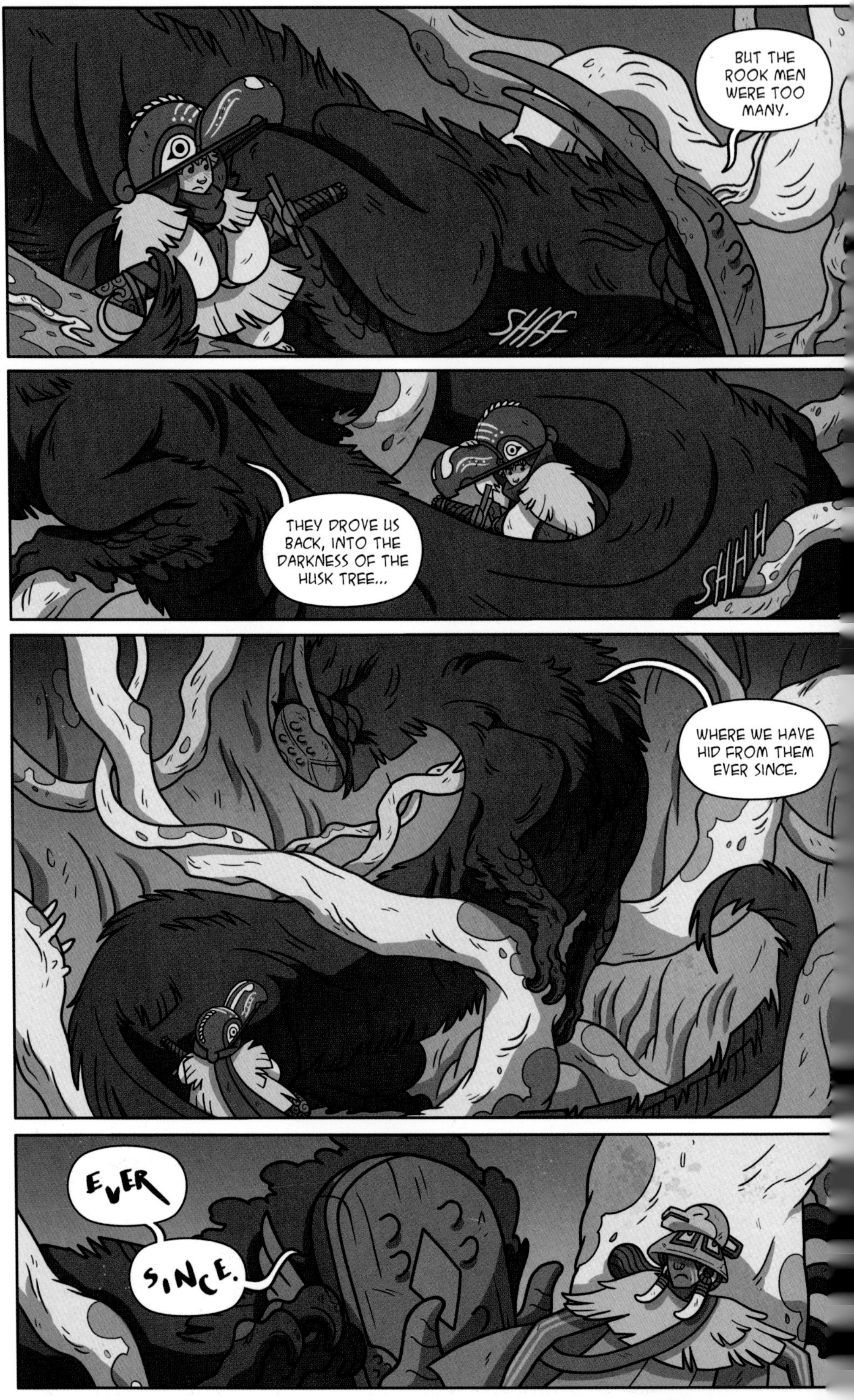
BUT THE ROOK MEN WERE TOO MANY.
SHFF
THEY DROVE US BACK, INTO THE DARKNESS OF THE HUSK TREE...
SHHH
WHERE WE HAVE HID FROM THEM EVER SINCE.
EVER
SINCE.

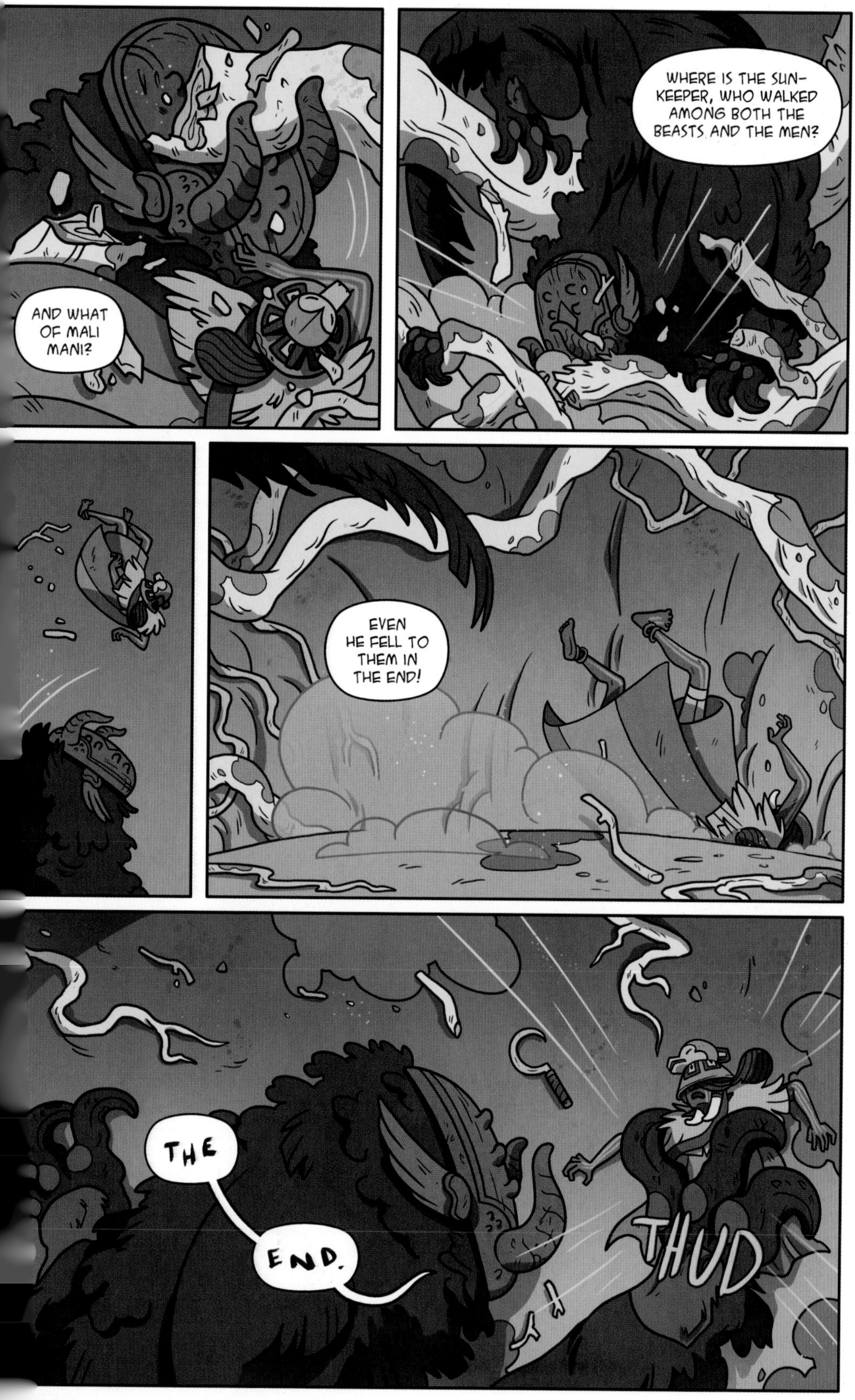
AND WHAT OF MALI MANI?
WHERE IS THE SUN-KEEPER, WHO WALKED AMONG BOTH THE BEASTS AND THE MEN?
EVEN HE FELL TO THEM IN THE END!
THE
END.
THUD

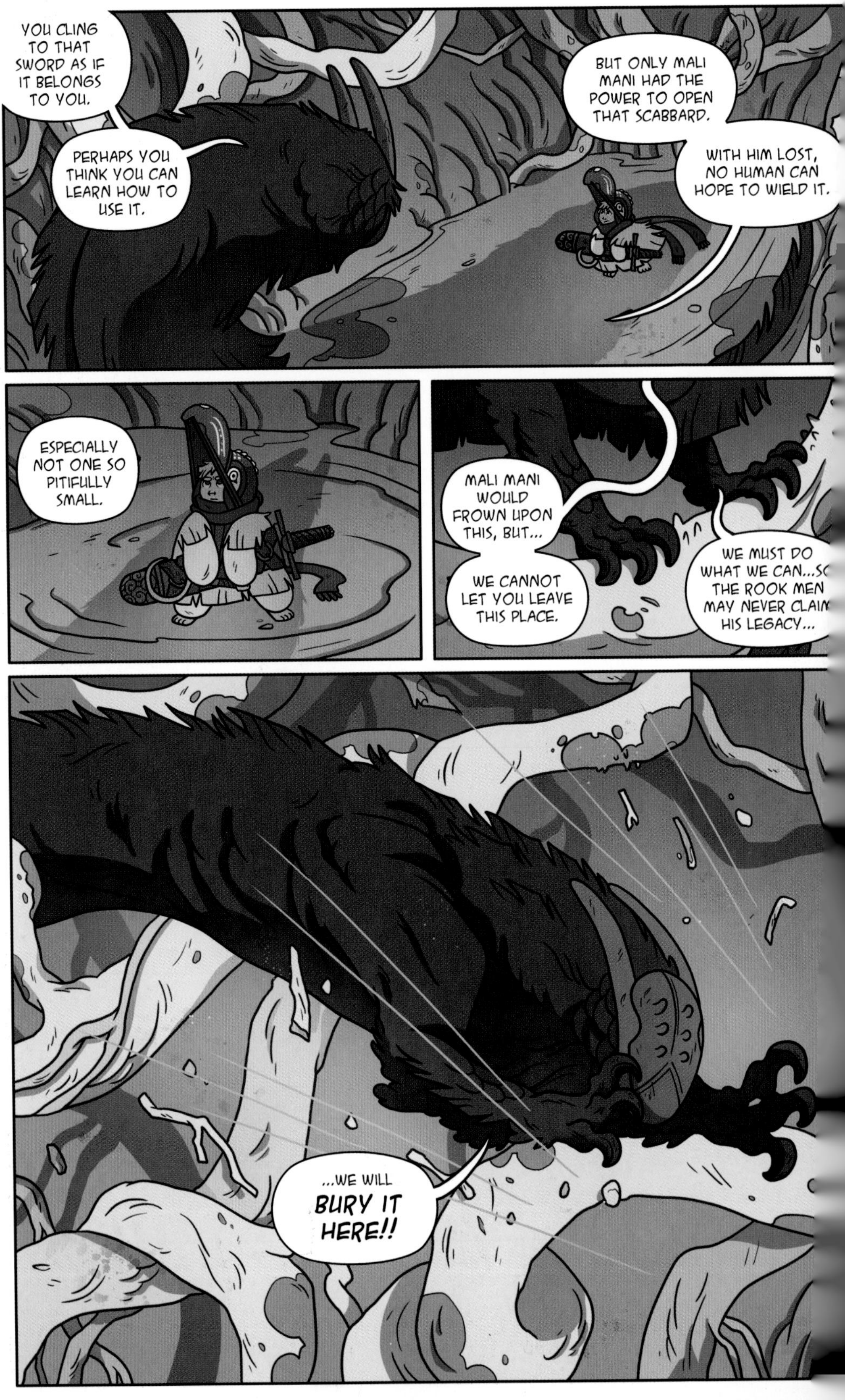
YOU CLING TO THAT SWORD AS IF IT BELONGS TO YOU.
PERHAPS YOU THINK YOU CAN LEARN HOW TO USE IT.
BUT ONLY MALI MANI HAD THE POWER TO OPEN THAT SCABBARD.
WITH HIM LOST, NO HUMAN CAN HOPE TO WIELD IT.
ESPECIALLY NOT ONE SO PITIFULLY SMALL.
MALI MANI WOULD FROWN UPON THIS, BUT...
WE CANNOT LET YOU LEAVE THIS PLACE.
WE MUST DO WHAT WE CAN...S
THE ROOK MEN MAY NEVER CLAI
HIS LEGACY...
...WE WILL BURY IT HERE!!

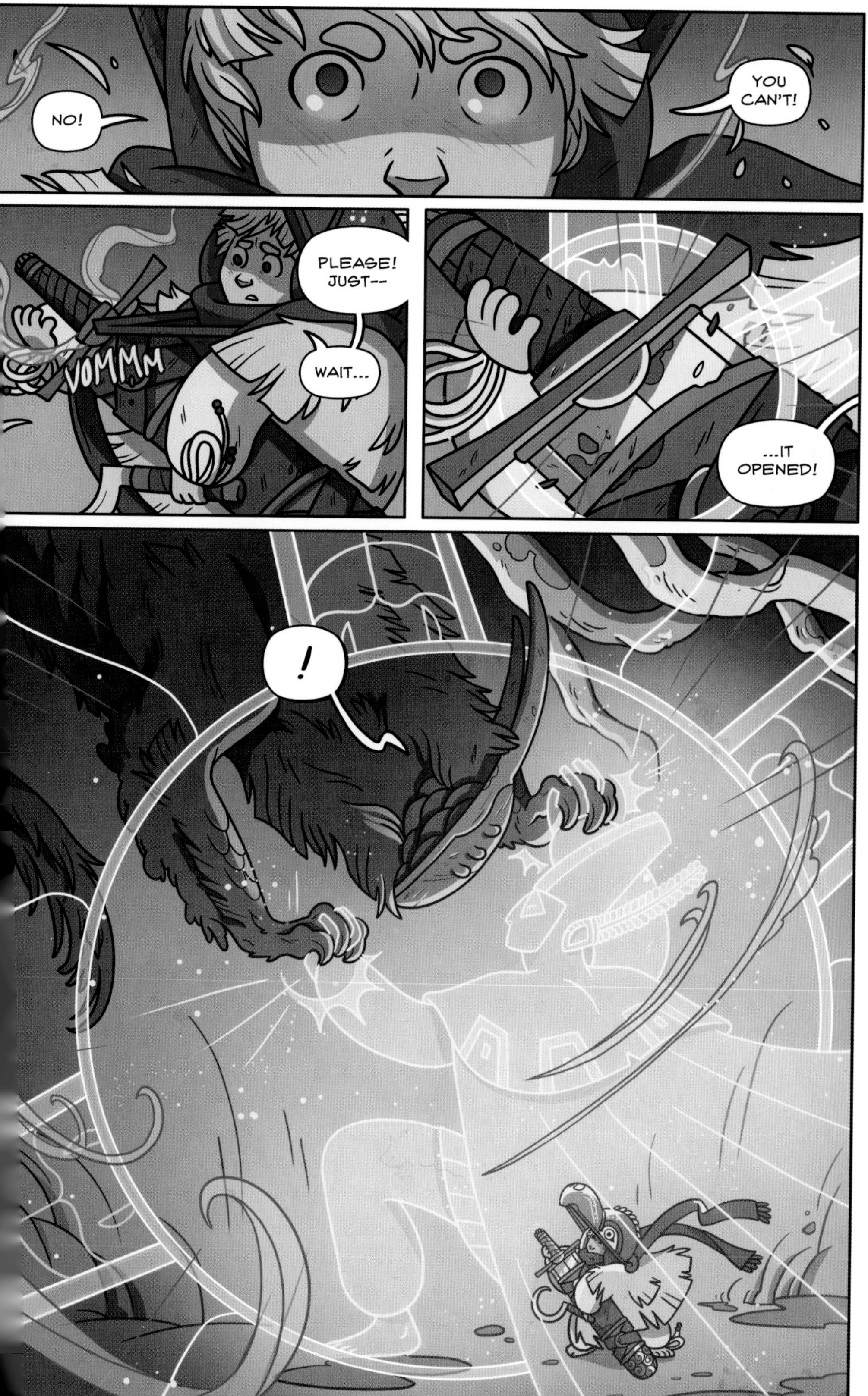
NO!
YOU CAN'T!
PLEASE! JUST--
VOMMM
WAIT...
...IT OPENED!
!

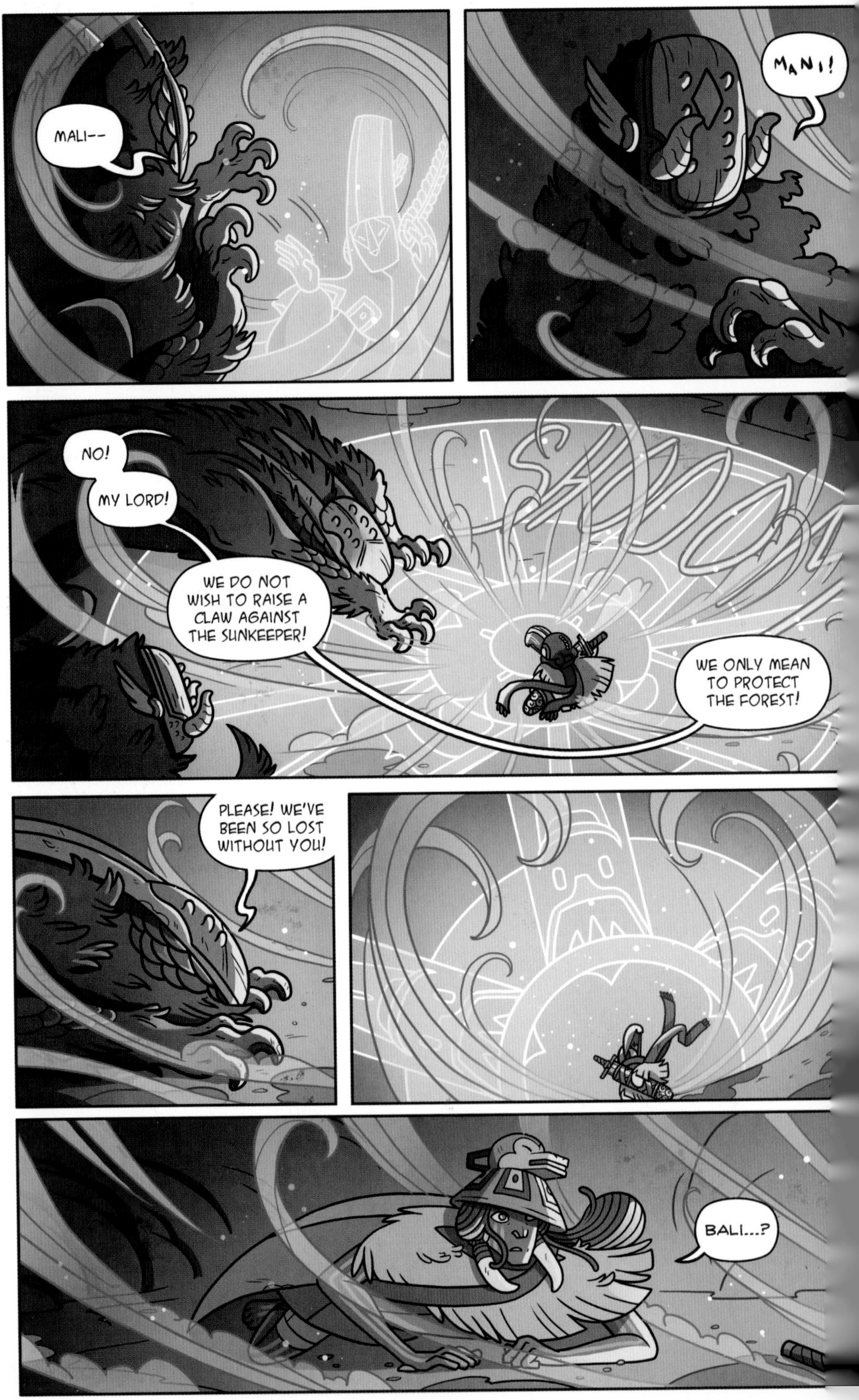
MALI--
MANI!
NO!
MY LORD!
WE DO NOT WISH TO RAISE A CLAW AGAINST THE SUNKEEPER!
WE ONLY MEAN TO PROTECT THE FOREST!
PLEASE! WE'VE BEEN SO LOST WITHOUT YOU!
BALI...?

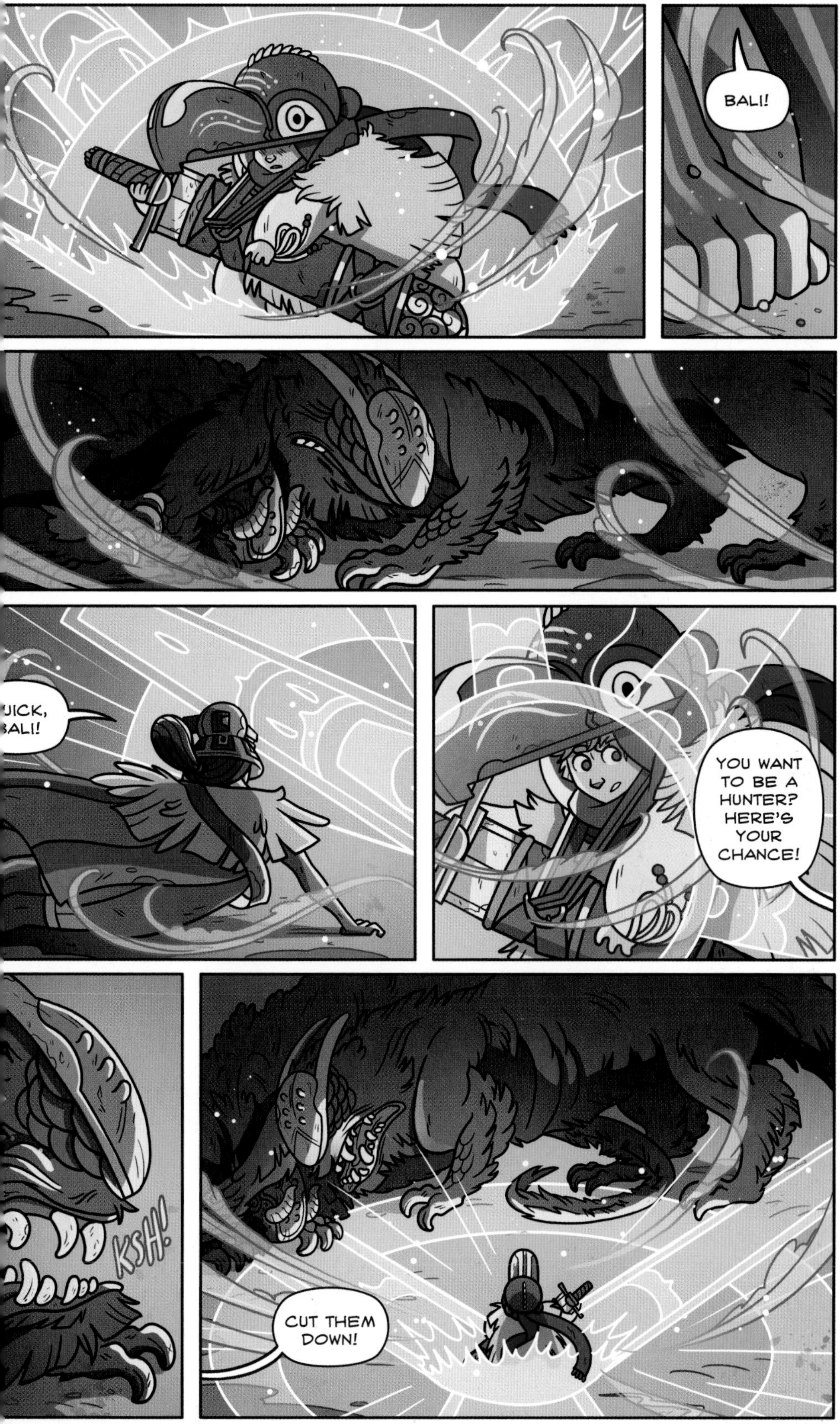
BALI!
UICK,
BALI!
YOU WANT TO BE A HUNTER? HERE'S YOUR CHANCE!
KSH!
CUT THEM DOWN!

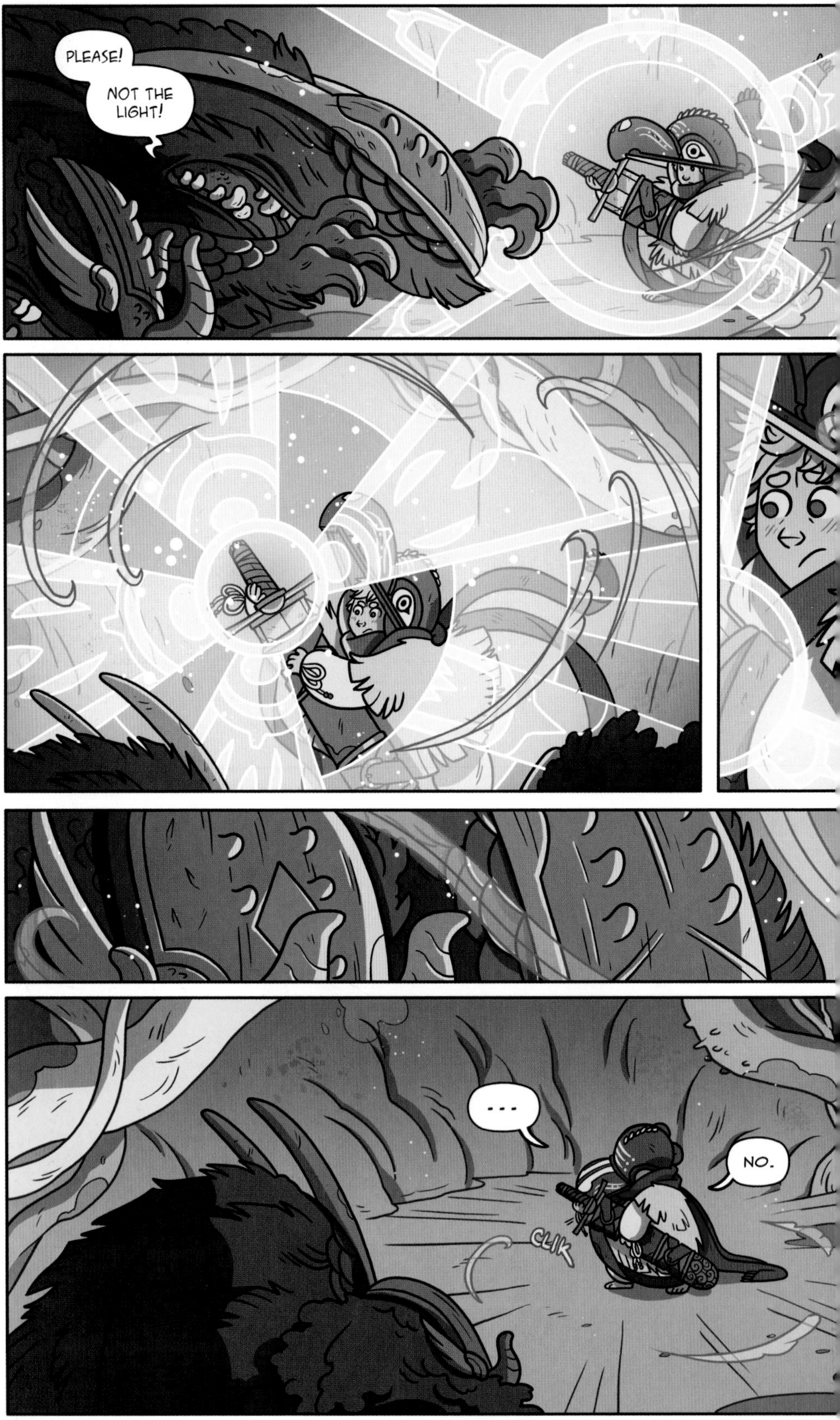
PLEASE!
NOT THE LIGHT!
...
NO.
CLIK

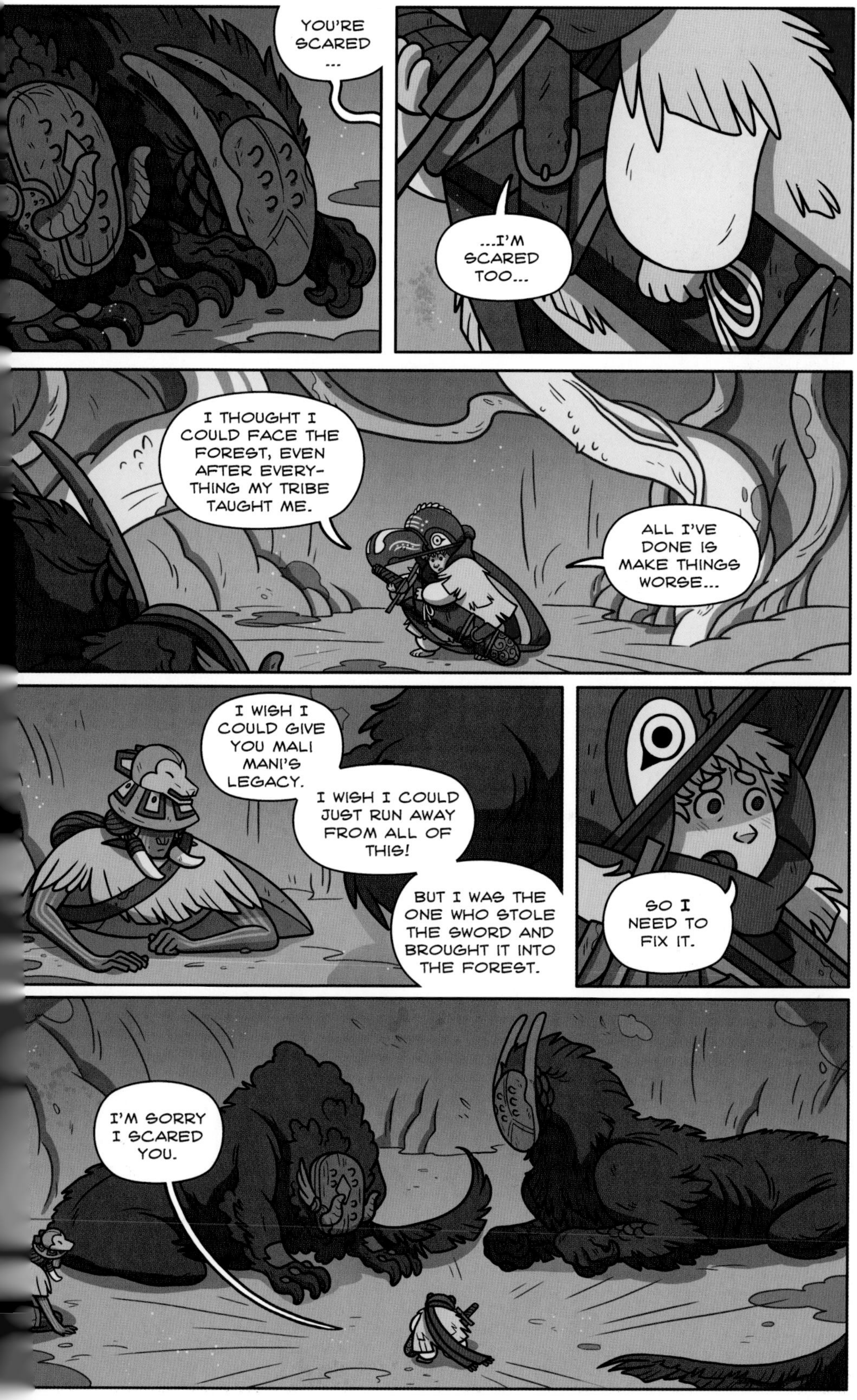
YOU'RE SCARED ...
...I'M SCARED TOO...
I THOUGHT I COULD FACE THE FOREST, EVEN AFTER EVERY-THING MY TRIBE TAUGHT ME.
ALL I'VE DONE IS MAKE THINGS WORSE...
I WISH I COULD GIVE YOU MALI MANI'S LEGACY.
I WISH I COULD JUST RUN AWAY FROM ALL OF THIS!
BUT I WAS THE ONE WHO STOLE THE SWORD AND BROUGHT IT INTO THE FOREST.
SO I NEED TO FIX IT.
I'M SORRY I SCARED YOU.

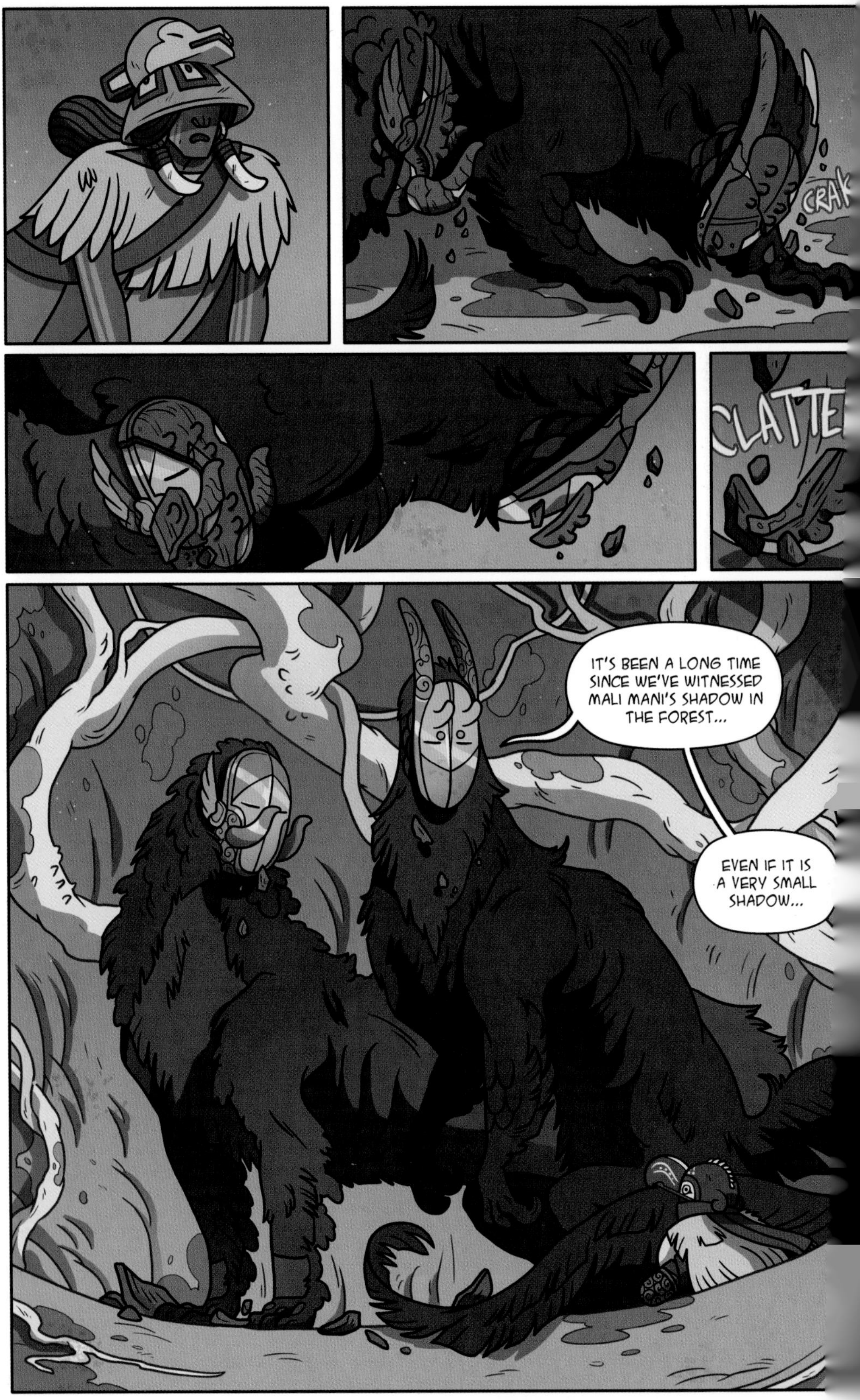
CRAK
CLATTE
IT'S BEEN A LONG TIME SINCE WE'VE WITNESSED MALI MANI'S SHADOW IN THE FOREST...
EVEN IF IT IS A VERY SMALL SHADOW...

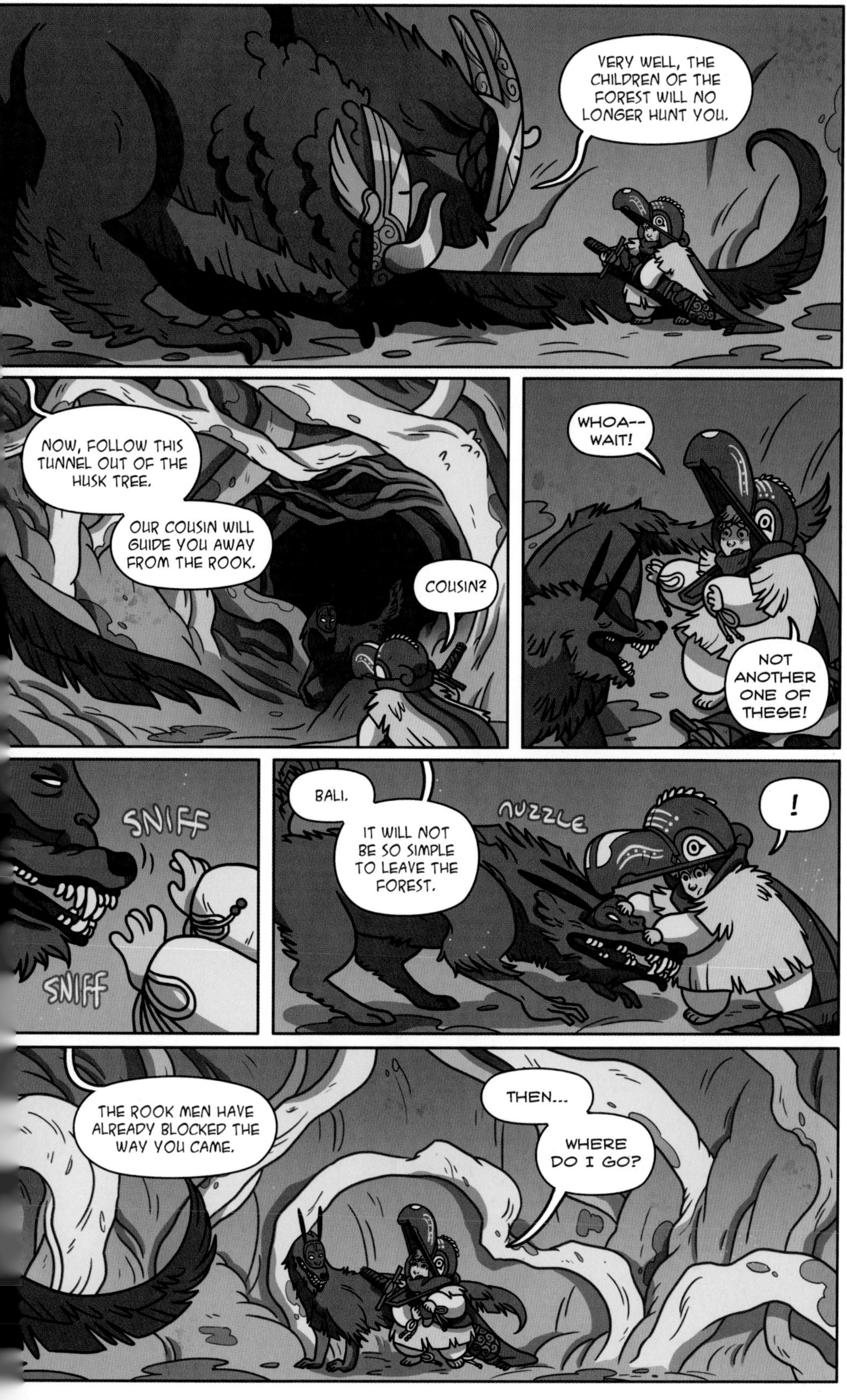
VERY WELL, THE CHILDREN OF THE FOREST WILL NO LONGER HUNT YOU.
NOW, FOLLOW THIS TUNNEL OUT OF THE HUSK TREE.
OUR COUSIN WILL GUIDE YOU AWAY FROM THE ROOK.
COUSIN?
WHOA--WAIT!
NOT ANOTHER ONE OF THESE!
SNIFF
SNIFF
BALI.
IT WILL NOT BE SO SIMPLE TO LEAVE THE FOREST.
NUZZLE
!
THE ROOK MEN HAVE ALREADY BLOCKED THE WAY YOU CAME.
THEN...
WHERE DO I GO?

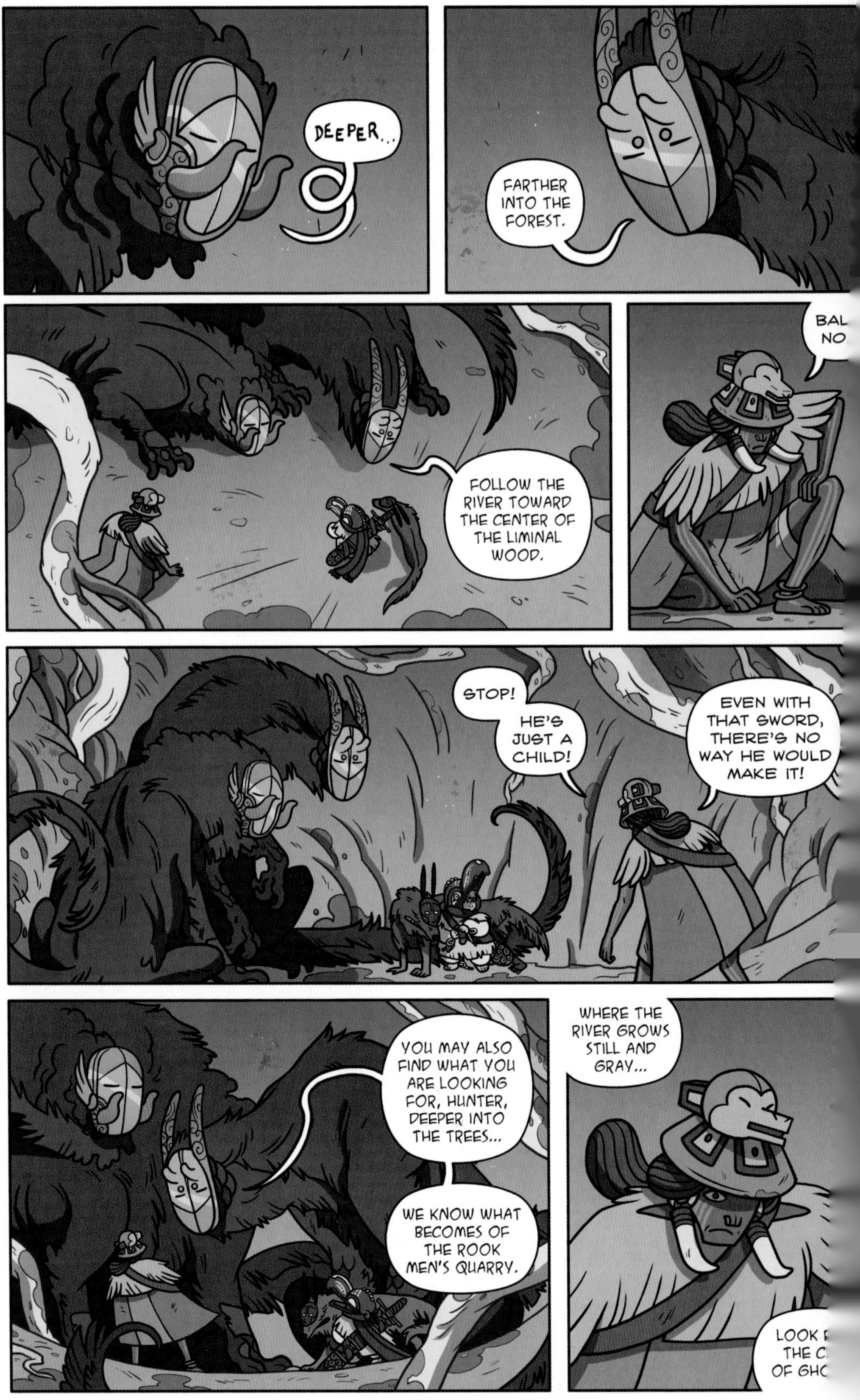
DEEPER...
FARTHER INTO THE FOREST.
FOLLOW THE RIVER TOWARD THE CENTER OF THE LIMINAL WOOD.
BAL NO
STOP!
HE'S JUST A CHILD!
EVEN WITH THAT SWORD, THERE'S NO WAY HE WOULD MAKE IT!
YOU MAY ALSO FIND WHAT YOU ARE LOOKING FOR, HUNTER, DEEPER INTO THE TREES...
WE KNOW WHAT BECOMES OF THE ROOK MEN'S QUARRY.
WHERE THE RIVER GROWS STILL AND GRAY...
LOOK THE OF

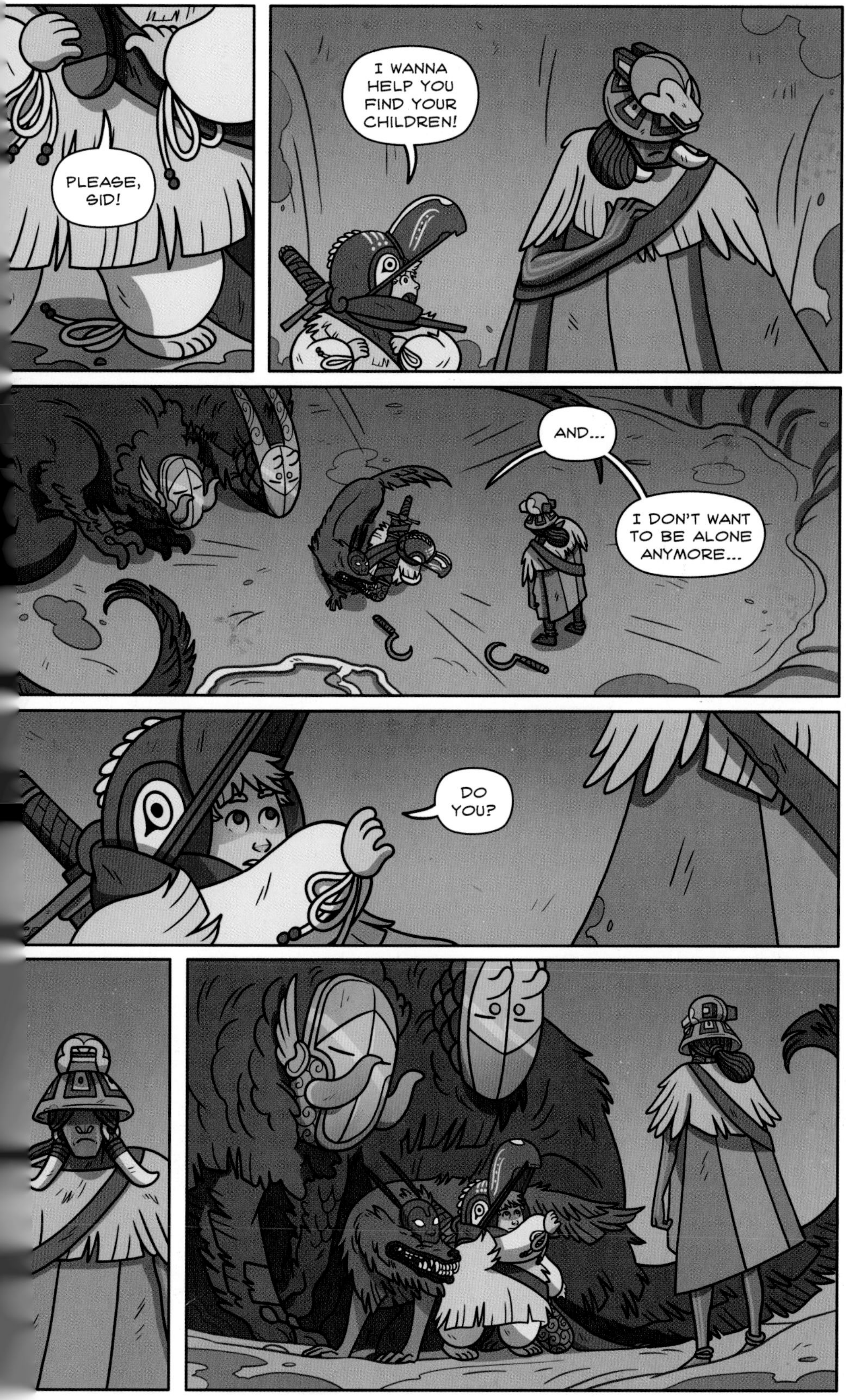

PLEASE, SID!
I WANNA HELP YOU FIND YOUR CHILDREN!
AND...
I DON'T WANT TO BE ALONE ANYMORE...
DO YOU?

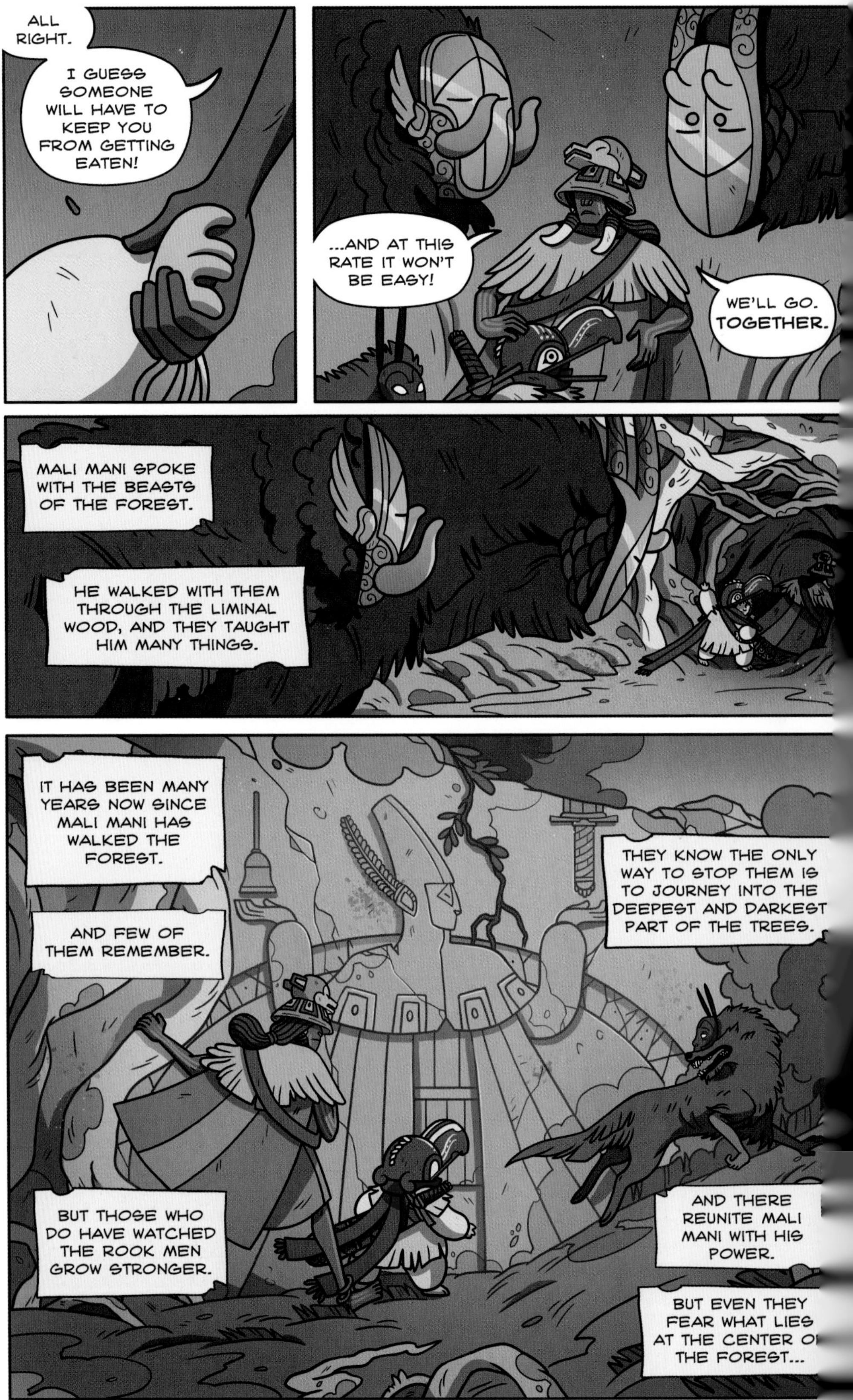
ALL RIGHT.
I GUESS SOMEONE WILL HAVE TO KEEP YOU FROM GETTING EATEN!
...AND AT THIS RATE IT WON'T BE EASY!
WE'LL GO. TOGETHER.
MALI MANI SPOKE WITH THE BEASTS OF THE FOREST.
HE WALKED WITH THEM THROUGH THE LIMINAL WOOD, AND THEY TAUGHT HIM MANY THINGS.
IT HAS BEEN MANY YEARS NOW SINCE MALI MANI HAS WALKED THE FOREST.
AND FEW OF THEM REMEMBER.
BUT THOSE WHO DO HAVE WATCHED THE ROOK MEN GROW STRONGER.
THEY KNOW THE ONLY WAY TO STOP THEM IS TO JOURNEY INTO THE DEEPEST AND DARKEST PART OF THE TREES.
AND THERE REUNITE MALI MANI WITH HIS POWER.
BUT EVEN THEY FEAR WHAT LIES AT THE CENTER O
THE FOREST...

TO BE CONT

BIRD·BOY

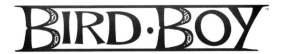

SKETCHBOOK

Notes by Anne Szabla

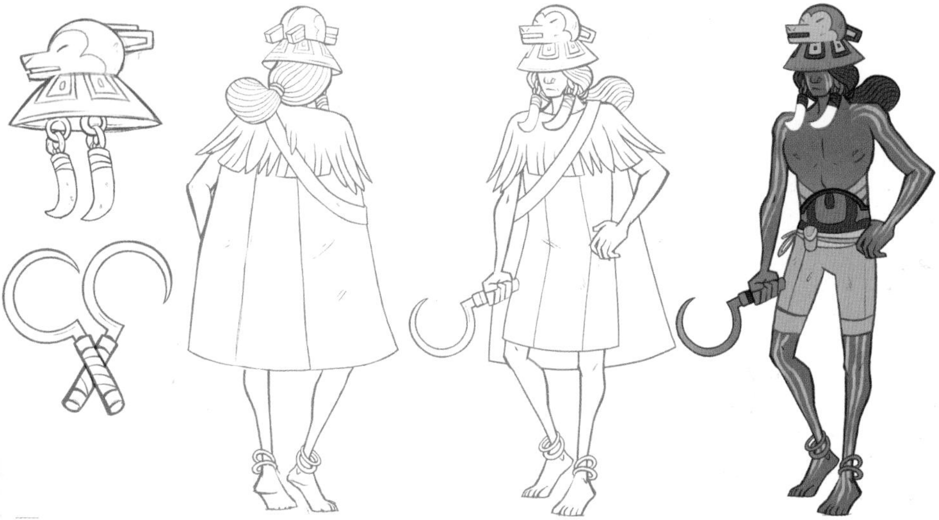

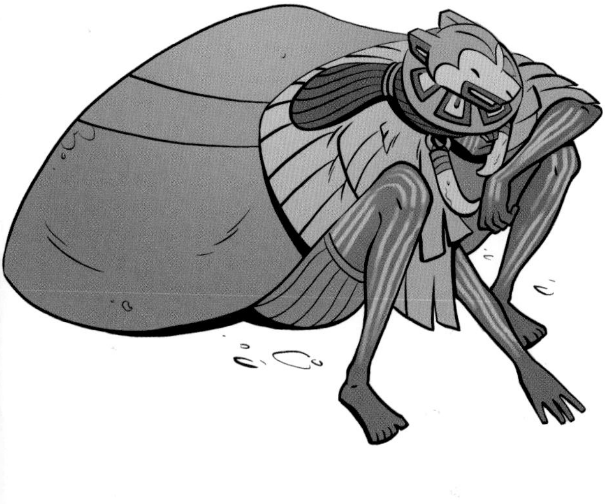

Designs for Sid!
I wanted to make him very tall and lean to contrast with how short and round Bali is.

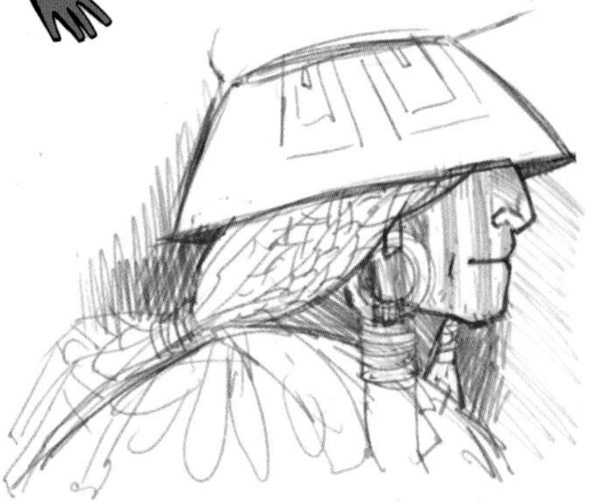

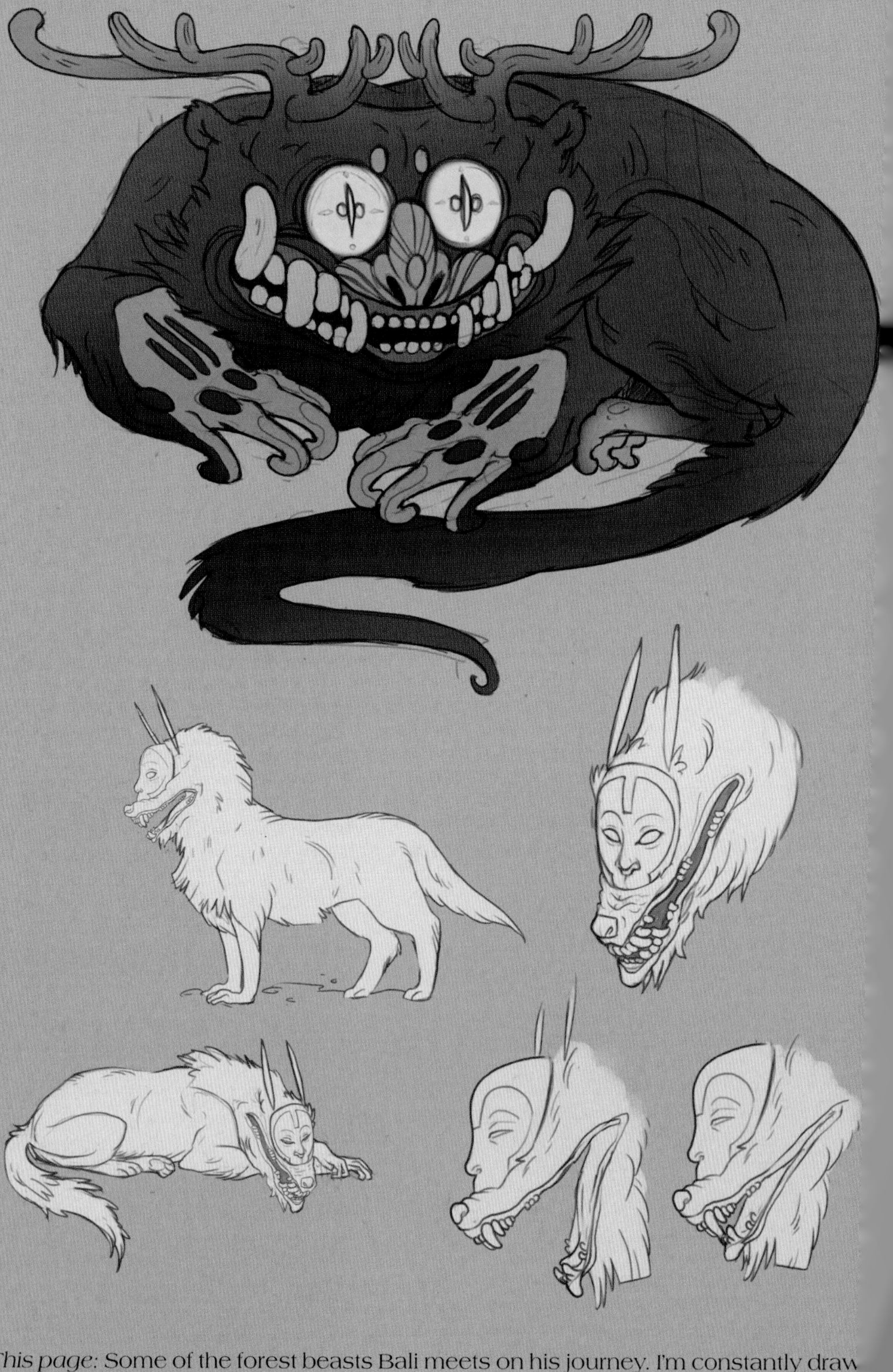

This page: Some of the forest beasts Bali meets on his journey. I'm constantly draw
weird creatures in my spare time. Sometimes when I know I need a creature for
comic I'll go back through my sketches and pick out one of my favorites. Other tir
a creature design will inspire a new part of a story and I'll purposefully write them
Facing: The web comic cover for Volume II.

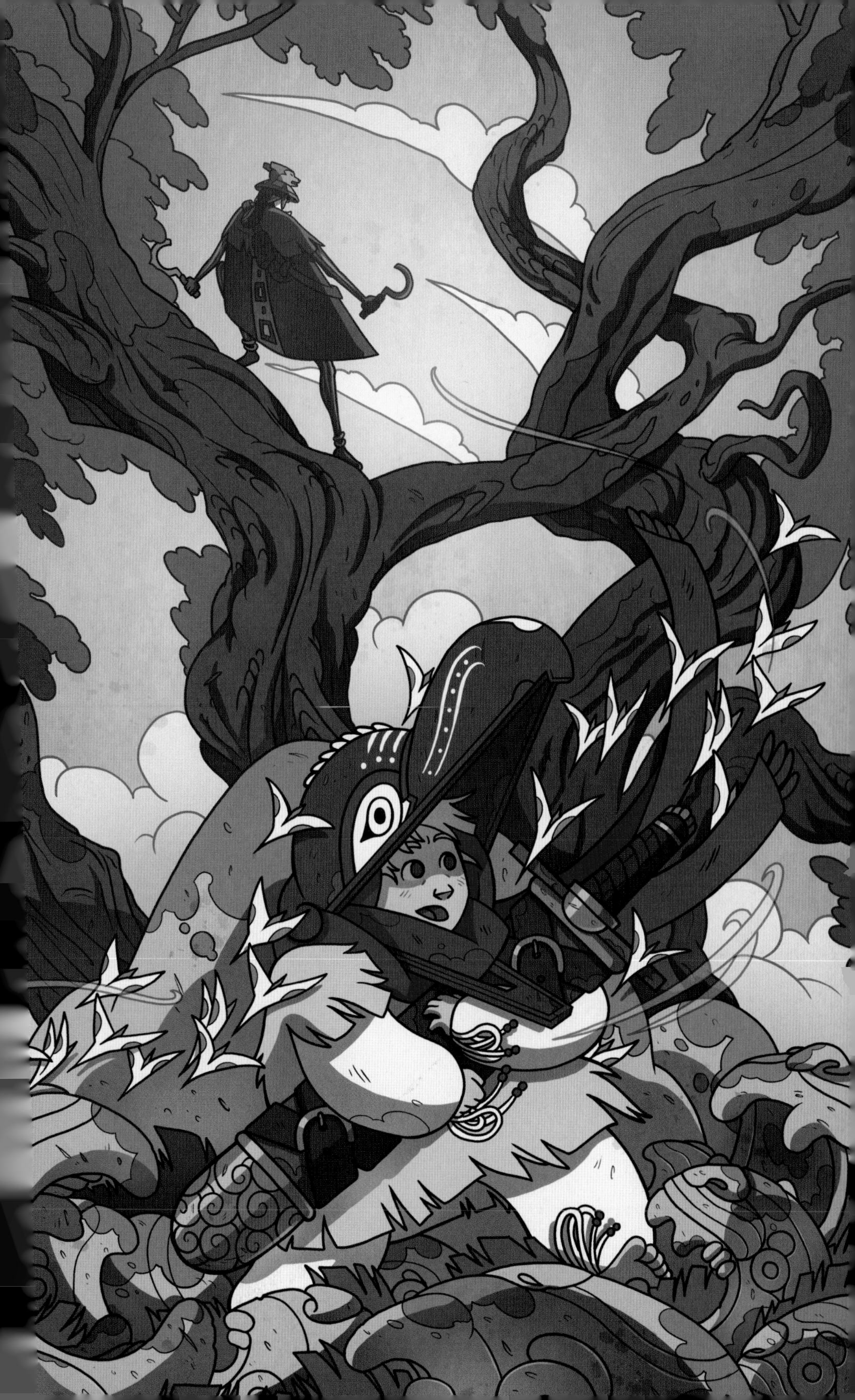

DISCOVER THE ADVENTURE!

Explore these beloved books
for the entire family.